I remember that Jane Jackson had hidden depths, even as an eighteen-year-old coed. When her parents died in that car accident, she made it through school by virtue of her grace and steely determination—the same qualities that drive her now as a hardworking single mom. Her classmate, Smith Parker, wasn't so lucky: when he was accused of stealing, his grades plummeted along with his confidence, costing him a college career. Now this Big Man on Campus is relegated to changing light bulbs as a Saunders University janitor.

But I haven't given up on Smith yet! Combining forces with Jane to help their favorite professor might be the way for them both to shake the past once and for all....

Dear Reader,

Well, it's September, which always sounds like a fresh start to me, no matter how old I get. And evidently we have six women this month who agree. In *Home Again* by Joan Elliott Pickart, a woman who can't have children has decided to work with them in a professional capacity—but when she is assigned an orphaned little boy, she fears she's in over her head. Then she meets his gorgeous guardian—and she's *sure* of it!

In the next installment of MOST LIKELY TO…, *The Measure of a Man* by Marie Ferrarella, a single mother attempting to help her beloved former professor joins forces with a former campus golden boy, now the college…custodian. What could have happened? Allison Leigh's *The Tycoon's Marriage Bid* pits a pregnant secretary against her ex-boss who, unbeknownst to him, has a real connection to her baby's father. In *The Other Side of Paradise* by Laurie Paige, next up in her SEVEN DEVILS miniseries, a mysterious woman seeking refuge as a ranch hand learns that she may have more ties to the community than she could have ever suspected. When a beautiful nurse is assigned to care for a devastatingly handsome, if cantankerous, cowboy, the results are…well, you get the picture—but you can have it spelled out for you in Stella Bagwell's next MEN OF THE WEST book, *Taming a Dark Horse*. And in *Undercover Nanny* by Wendy Warren, a domestically challenged female detective decides it's necessary to penetrate the lair of single father and heir to a grocery fortune by pretending to be…his nanny. Hmm. It *could* work.…

So enjoy, and snuggle up. Fall weather is just around the corner.…

Happy reading!

Gail Chasan
Senior Editor

Please address questions and book requests to:
Silhouette Reader Service
U.S.: 3010 Walden Ave., P.O. Box 1325, Buffalo, NY 14269
Canadian: P.O. Box 609, Fort Erie, Ont. L2A 5X3

THE
MEASURE
OF A MAN

MARIE FERRARELLA

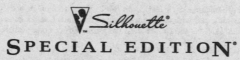

Silhouette®

SPECIAL EDITION®

Published by Silhouette Books

America's Publisher of Contemporary Romance

Special thanks and acknowledgment are given
to Marie Ferrarella for her contribution
to the MOST LIKELY TO... series.

To
Susan Litman, who kept her cool
while coordinating six authors

 SILHOUETTE BOOKS

ISBN 0-373-24706-0

THE MEASURE OF A MAN

Copyright © 2005 by Harlequin Books S.A.

Visit Silhouette Books at www.eHarlequin.com

Printed in U.S.A.

Books by Marie Ferrarella in Miniseries

MARIE FERRARELLA

This RITA® Award-winning author has written over one hundred and fifty books for Silhouette, some under the name Marie Nicole. Her romances are beloved by fans worldwide.

Dear Jane,

I bet you can't count the number of times I caught you looking my way in our English class! Just kidding—I'm flattered. Who wouldn't be—you're the prettiest girl in the room. If I'm in town over the summer, I'll look you up—maybe we can get together sometime and talk about Shakespeare.

Your friend,

Smith

Chapter One

"I miss you, Mary." Professor Gilbert Harrison sighed, feeling the ache go deep into his chest like a long, sharp serrated knife. "I miss your beautiful smile."

Standing in his cluttered second-floor office at Saunders University, his hands clasped helplessly behind his back, the professor gazed at the framed photograph of his late wife, which sat on his bookshelf.

Wedged in between stacks of books he'd long since forgotten about, it was the photograph he had taken of Mary about a year after they'd gotten married. In it she was young, vibrant, with the joy of life sparkling in her eyes. It reflected the woman he had locked in his heart. Mary, the way he always pictured her each time his mind summoned her image. And Gilbert summoned that image as often as there were hours in the day.

Even now, eight months after she'd died so suddenly of a heart ailment neither one of them had known she'd had, leaving him to face the world on his own, hardly an hour went by when something didn't bring his thoughts back to her.

He'd never really been aware of just how much he depended on her, just how much his sweet, quiet, steadfast Mary had been his rock, his haven, when times were bad. Just having her to come home to had been a comfort.

There was no such comfort available to him now.

And soon, he thought sadly, there might not even be a home, for he lived just off the campus in a cozy two-story house provided by the university.

What the university giveth, it taketh away, he thought without humor. And because of Alexander Broadstreet, the board of directors seemed bent on taking away his job as swiftly as it could.

"They're trying to get rid of me, Mary," he told the photograph sadly. "Trying to squeeze me out." He'd sensed it for a while now, tried not to think about it. But the efforts had gone into high gear since he'd failed to take any of the "hints" thrown his way. They used excuses, saying things like "early retirement" and perhaps he should look into taking an extended sabbatical abroad. But he knew what they were really saying. "Get ye gone." Gilbert sighed, shaking his head. "Extended sabbatical abroad. What would I ever do abroad by myself? All I ever wanted to do was to stay here, to teach and do some good. And be with you."

Staring at the photograph again, he ran his hand over

his full mane of dark graying hair. "I'm tired, Mary. For two cents, I'd go—if you were still here to go along with me. But you're not, and this is all I've ever known how to do." He raised his chin proudly, struggling to remain the fighter he knew his wife would have wanted him to be. "Besides, I'm not some doddering octogenarian, I'm only fifty-eight. Fifty-eight," he repeated more heatedly. "And I've still got a lot left to give to the university. To the students."

And then he frowned, a glint hardening his eyes. Besides he was not about to give Alex Broadstreet the satisfaction of giving him the bum's rush. Gilbert Harrison had been at Saunders long before Broadstreet, and he planned on being there long after the board of directors asked Broadstreet to leave. The satisfaction in that image made him smile at the photo. "Try to get rid of me, will he? We'll show him, right? Right?"

His words echoed back to him, absorbed by the dust and clutter in the room that had basically been the same since he'd taken it thirty-one years ago.

Gilbert suddenly felt old, despite his words. He felt not unlike the fictional Don Quixote, tilting at windmills and sensing the futility of it deep in his bones.

"Oh, Lord, I wish you were here, Mary. You always knew what to do, what to say, to make me feel better. Even when things were darkest." An ironic smile curved his lips.

Reaching out, he traced his fingertips along the glass that separated him from the face he loved, wishing he could touch her just one more time. Have her look at him like that just once more.

"You were always the person I could turn to." And then, as it always did, that nagging little voice from deep inside of him whispered recriminatingly in his head. His one indiscretion weighed heavily on him as always. Mary had never known, but that didn't lessen the guilt. It was not something he was proud of.

He sighed. Thank God she'd never found out. He would have rather died than to ever hurt Mary. And then an ironic smile slipped over his lips. "Of course, you know now, don't you? You're in the position to know everything now." He blinked, his shame for the affair a burden he'd never lost despite the years he spent trying to make it up to his wife.

He resumed pacing, careful to avoid knocking over any of the files on the floor. In some places they were stacked calf-high. Maybe his current troubles were payback, then. Except, somehow, he couldn't bring himself to think of Mary as being vengeful in the afterlife.

At the window now, he looked out onto the rolling green of the campus. Soon it would be filled with students again, another year beginning. A year he meant to be a part of.

Even as he sought to cleave to the thought of surviving this game the board was playing with him, his thoughts turned to Broadstreet, the man who was spearheading the none-too-secret campaign to oust him. What had Broadstreet called him in one of his arguments? Old-fashioned, that was it.

Gilbert looked over his shoulder to his wife's picture again. "Old-fashioned, Mary. They're saying I'm too old-fashioned. As if caring and compassion, seeing the student, not the grade, was something that had fallen out of favor. When did it stop being about learning?" The sigh that came this time as he shook his head was from deep inside his soul.

Just as he uttered his concern, Gilbert heard a polite cough behind him. Ordinarily, Gilbert would have expected to see a student standing on the threshold of his office. The number of students who had come into his office in the last thirty years, seeking his advice, was legion. He'd long since stopped counting. But in the past six months, there had been fewer and fewer, as if this student body somehow sensed that he was now considered a pariah in the scheme of things and to be associated with him meant tying yourself to not a shooting star, but to a sun that was about to go nova at any moment.

The office door creaked as Jane Jackson closed it behind her. She stood looking at the professor a little uncertainly. A moment earlier, her pale green eyes had swiftly swept around the almost-claustrophobic room, looking for whoever the professor was talking to. There were stacks of books and files on every available surface, as well as on the floor surrounding the scarred desk, like some pint-size invaders. But no person or persons were on the receiving end of the professor's words.

"I didn't mean to interrupt, Professor." Who *had* he been talking to? She brought her eyes back to him and, because she felt close to him, said the obvious. "You're alone."

It wasn't a question. Unless he'd acquired some small pet she couldn't see because of the clutter, Professor Harrison was very much alone in the room.

Turning from the bookshelf, the professor smiled at her warmly. "Not alone anymore, now that you're here."

"But I heard you talking..."

Jane let her voice trail off, not wanting to upset him or to sound accusatory. It was obvious that he'd been talking to himself. Extensively. She'd heard the sound of his voice as she'd approached from her own office located across the way from his. Ever since the professor's wife had died, he'd become a little more eccentric and she worried about him, about the state of his mind. He and Mrs. Harrison had been married for decades. So unlike her own marriage, Jane thought ruefully.

She'd long since come to think of Professor Harrison as a surrogate father. Having lost both her parents in her freshman year at Saunders University, she'd found herself at emotional, not to mention financial, loose ends. The financial dilemma had been mysteriously resolved when she'd received a letter from the university's administration office telling her that her tuition for the remaining three years at Saunders had been paid for and that some money had been set aside for her living expenses, as well. She'd never found out where the money had come from and had spent the first year convinced that there had been some mistake, praying that it wouldn't come to light until after she graduated.

As for emotionally, that had been an even greater dilemma. She'd been an only child of only children. There was no one for her to turn to. Being shy, there was no network of friends, either. She was utterly alone, isolated. And having very dangerous thoughts about the futility of life. At the time, Professor Harrison had been her English teacher. But he'd become so much more.

He'd found her crying on the steps of the library shortly after her parents' funeral, feeling hopelessly lost and alone. Very quietly, very gently, he'd expressed his sympathies and extended an open invitation to her to come see him in his office anytime she needed to talk. At first, she'd hesitated, but slowly found herself taking him up on his offer. And feeling the better for it.

Even so, that first Christmas after her parents' death, when almost everyone at the university had gone home for the holidays, she knew she would have expired from loneliness if the professor hadn't insisted that she spend them with him and his wife.

As far as she was concerned, he'd saved her life. Professor Harrison had literally been her lifeline back to the world of the living and she wanted desperately to return the favor any way she could.

But at times it was hard to reach him in his grief.

Gilbert smiled at Jane. She was twenty-nine years old, but he still thought of her as a young girl. Time moved by too quickly. His Mary had been very fond of Jane. Very upset, too, when the girl had suddenly announced that she was to marry Drew Walters.

"He's no good for her, Gil, but she's too blind with love to see," Mary had sighed.

"Maybe it'll work out," he remembered saying, and Mary had looked at him with that smile of hers. The one that said she knew better.

She'd patted his face and brushed a kiss across his cheek. "Oh, Gil, you like to see the best in everyone, but some people don't have a best. Or if they do, they don't try to live up to it."

And, as usual, Mary had been right. Drew Walters had turned out to be as shallow as he was handsome. The rumor was that Walters had run around on Jane almost from the very beginning of their short, tumultuous marriage.

Gilbert nodded at the photograph on the bookshelf. "I was just talking things over with Mary."

Jane nodded knowingly, glancing at the photograph. "And what did she say to you?"

"To fight." The professor squared his shoulders unconsciously.

Jane forced a smile to her lips as she nodded again. She was determined not to show the professor just how worried she was about this skirmish between him and the board. It bothered her that a selfish note had entered into this, but she couldn't help being worried, not just for him, but for herself, as well. Because if they forced the professor into early retirement, or worse, made him so angry that he resigned, there would be no place for her here, either. She was Professor Gilbert Harrison's personal assistant and secretary. If he was persona non grata, then so was she. Anyone coming in to take his place would bring his or her own secretary with them.

Not that she could see herself working for anyone who usurped Professor Harrison. But she did need a job. Desperately. Drew had left her with next to nothing when he'd disappeared.

Jane inclined her head toward the professor's photograph of his wife. "Mrs. Harrison was always a fighter."

He was unaware of his sigh as he struggled against the sharp sting of longing. "Yes, she was."

Noting the signs of impending sadness, Jane did what she could to rally the professor's spirits. "And she would have told Alexander Broadstreet just what she thought of him."

At that, she succeeded in getting Gilbert to laugh. "My Mary was first and foremost a lady, Janie." He turned from the photograph. "She would have never used four-letter words to describe anyone."

"Maybe not," Jane allowed with a smile. "But Broadstreet would have gotten the message. Mrs. Harrison would have let her eyes do her talking for her."

Envisioning a scene between his fiercely loyal wife and the sharp-featured Broadstreet, Gilbert chuckled. Mary had never liked Broadstreet. "That she would have." And then, because he knew he had to keep on pushing forward, no matter how hard it felt, Gilbert turned toward his former student and asked, "So, did you come by to ask me something?"

"Just that I'm going to lunch and I wanted to know if I could bring you back anything."

He smiled wistfully at her. "Yes, the last thirty years." He was almost half serious as he added, "I'd like to live them all again."

Jane patted his arm, hoping that she sounded at least a little convincing as she said, "The next thirty will even be better."

"Not if Broadstreet has his way."

Jane attempted to give him a confident look, the way she used to see Mrs. Harrison do. "Then we'll just have to make sure that Broadstreet doesn't win, won't we?"

Genuine concern entered his eyes as he looked at her. "Jane, I don't want you getting into any trouble on my account."

"Believe me, Professor, I couldn't think of a nobler cause to undertake than to make sure that you remain with the university for as long as you want to," she said firmly. "And even longer than that," Jane added with a smile. What would she have done without him? And she wasn't the only one. She knew of a great many students who had come to feel the same over the years. "There are still lots of students who could benefit from your advice, your wisdom and your kindness."

He couldn't help but laugh at her serious tone and the look on her face. Bless the girl, she really had helped raise his spirits. "My God, Jane, I feel as if I've just been eavesdropping on my own eulogy."

"Bite your tongue," she told him. Death was something she didn't like to even joke about. "Not for many, many years to come." Pushing the thought away, she summoned as serene an expression as she could and asked, "Now then, can I bring you back a roast beef sandwich from the Sandwich Bar?"

The Sandwich Bar was little more than an afterthought beside the campus bookstore, quite apart from the main cafeteria and the two food court areas that were on opposite ends of the campus. But it served the best sandwiches around and she had been going there for the last year. Since the prices were more than reasonable, it was her one indulgence for herself: not to have to brown bag it, with leftovers every day.

"French dipped," she prodded. "Just the way you like it."

Since Mary had died, his appetite had been less than stellar. There were times that he went from one end of the day to the other without eating. There was no rumbling stomach to remind him, no hunger at all. Apparently, Jane had taken keeping his strength up upon herself, too.

He shook his head. "You're trying to take care of me."

She saw no reason to deny it. She wanted him to know how much he mattered, not just to her but to so many of them. With his wife's death and now this campaign to be rid of him, she was afraid his once-indomitable spirit would be killed entirely.

"Doing my damnedest, Professor." She shifted so that her feet were firmly planted on the worn carpet. "I'm not leaving until you place your order."

"All right, Janie, you win." So saying, Gilbert put his hand first into one pocket, then another, until he located his wallet. He pulled it out and looked through the bills.

"No," Jane protested, pushing his wallet back, "it's on me."

He gave her a steely look that was meant to penetrate down to her soul. "Young lady, I know for a fact that you can barely afford your own lunch, much less pay for mine." Taking out a twenty, he pressed it into her palm. "Here, this should cover us both." He saw the protest rising to her lips and headed it off. "Please, Jane, allow me a few pleasures."

Reluctantly she closed her hand over the bill, then brushed a quick kiss against his cheek. How could they possibly be thinking of getting rid of him? It was Broadstreet who should be getting his walking papers, not the professor. And as quickly as possible.

"You really are a dear, dear man," she told him affectionately.

Sinking into the leather chair that welcomed him like an old friend, Gilbert waved her away, his attention already directed toward the open file on his desk. The university had long since removed him from the English department and he no longer coached a baseball team the way he had in the old days. But they had allowed him to continue in the capacity of adviser and counselor and he took his work and the students that went with it very, very seriously.

It meant he could still help the deserving. The way he'd been doing, one way or another, for the last thirty years.

For a second longer, Jane stood watching him.

Damn them all to hell, she thought angrily. How dare they threaten to put that wonderful man out to pasture? Without his wife, all Professor Harrison had was his work here at the university. She knew in her heart that if he was forced into retirement, the man who had been like a father to her would, in a very short period of time, certainly whither away and die.

She wasn't about to let that happen—even if it wouldn't impact her own financial situation the way it would. Not while there was a single breath left in her body.

Angry, wishing she could get her hands around Broadstreet's throat and squeeze it until the man promised to leave the professor alone, Jane turned on her heel and swung open the outer office door. She did it with the same amount of force she would have delivered to Broadstreet's solar plexus if she were given to street brawling.

She heard the creaking noise at the same time she shut the door behind her.

The ladder hadn't been there when she'd walked into the professor's office.

If it had, it would have blocked her access. As it was now, the door had come in jolting contact with the side of the wide, ten-foot ladder. Jolting as well the man who was perched two rungs from the top.

Momentarily stunned, Jane reacted automatically. Being the mother of one very hyper five-year-old had trained her to be prepared for anything and to react to situations even when she was half asleep or caught completely off guard, the way she was now. That was why the saleswoman at the department store last month hadn't been smacked over the head by a mannequin that would have fallen right on her head if Jane hadn't caught it in time. And why the maintenance man changing the light bulb didn't go flying off the tottering ladder now.

Her legs braced, Jane grabbed both sides of the ladder that were facing her, pulling back with all her might and steadying it so that the ladder didn't go over on its side.

The next minute its rather well-built, muscled occupant was all but sliding down the steps, eager to do so on his own power rather than because of gravity. Inches apart, his hand on the rungs to ground the ladder, his temper flashed as he glared at the cause of his sudden earthquake.

"Damn it, why don't you watch where you're going?" he demanded.

She'd once been timid and shy. But life and the professor had taught her that she needed to stand up for herself or face being stepped on. She was in no mood to be stepped on.

Jane met the man's glare with one of her own. "Why don't you watch where you're sticking your ladder? Don't you know any better than to put it so close to a door?"

Chapter Two

Nothing irritated Smith Parker more than being in the wrong. The way he was now. He frowned deeply. Not at the woman in front of him, but at the situation. This was not where he expected to be at this point in his life.

At twenty-nine, Smith had expected to be doing something important. At the very least, something more significant than changing light bulbs in the hallway of one of the older buildings at the very same university he'd once attended, nurturing such wonderful dreams of his future.

A future that definitely did *not* include a maintenance uniform. But this was the same university that had abruptly turned his life upside down, stripped him of his scholarship, money awarded through a work-study program, and thus his ability to pay for the education that would have seen him rise above a life involving only menial jobs.

An education that would have allowed him to become something more than he was now destined to be.

In a way, Smith supposed that he should be grateful he was working, grateful that he was anywhere at all. There had been a stretch of time, right after he'd spiraled down emotionally and sleepwalked through his exams, causing his grades to drop and him to leave the university, that he had seriously considered giving up everything and meeting oblivion.

Ultimately it was his love for his parents who had loved him and stood by him with unwavering faith throughout it all, that had kept him from doing anything drastic. Anything permanent. He knew that ending his own life would in effect end theirs.

So he had pulled back from the very brink of self-destruction, reassessed his situation and tried to figure out what he could do with himself.

The answer was just to pass from one day to the next, drifting without a plan, he who had once entertained so many ideas.

To support himself and not wind up as a blot on society's conscience, he'd taken on a variety of dead-end, lackluster jobs, doing his best but leaving his heart out of it. Some of the others he worked with felt that a job well done was its own reward, but he didn't. He did them because that was what he was getting paid for, nothing else. He did them well because that was his nature, but one position was pretty much like another. When his father's health had begun to fail, any tiny speck of hope he'd still entertained about eventually returning to college died. He'd needed to help out financially.

When this unsolicited offer had arrived out of the blue, asking him to come down to the university to apply for the position that began at something higher than minimum wage, he'd taken it only because of the money. There had been no joy in it, no secret setting down of goals for himself to achieve anything beyond what he was offered.

He was seriously convinced that, for him, there was no joy left in anything. Being accused of something he had not done and verbally convicted without being allowed to defend himself had killed his spirit.

So he did his work, making sure that he was never remiss, never in a position to be found lacking by anyone ever again.

But today, his mind had wandered. Just before beginning his round of small, tedious chores, he'd seen a landscaping truck go by. The truck's logo proclaimed it to belong to a local family company that had been in business for the past fifteen years. Seeing it had momentarily catapulted him into the past.

That had been his goal once. To have a business of his own. Something where he was his own master, making his own hours, responsible for his own success. Evaluated and held to high standards by his own measure, not whimsically made to live up to someone else's, someone who might, for whatever reason, find him lacking through no fault of his own but because of something they themselves were dealing with.

The truck had driven around the corner and disappeared. Just as his dreams had.

He'd returned to his chores in a dark frame of mind. Even so, he went through the paces, giving a hundred percent, no more, no less.

He'd spent most of the morning dealing with a clogged drain incapacitating the university's indoor pool. The smell of stagnant water was still in his head if not physically with him and admittedly he wasn't exactly in the best frame of mind, even though he was tackling a far lesser problem.

So he hadn't been paying attention when he set up the ladder and worked the defunct bulb out of the socket in the ceiling. He'd only used the ladder instead of the extension pole he normally employed because someone had apparently made off with the pole.

Even the hallowed halls of Saunders saw theft, he'd thought.

It seemed ironic, given that was the offense he'd been accused of all those many years ago. Theft. When he discovered that the pole, an inexpensive thirty-dollar item, was missing, he couldn't help wondering if this would somehow come back to haunt him. Would the head of the maintenance department think he'd taken it for some obscure reason?

Once a thief...

Except that he hadn't been. Not even that one time he'd been accused by that pompous, self-centered jerk, Jacob Weber.

Smith looked down now at Jane Jackson's face, biting back a stinging retort that was born of defensiveness and the less-than-stellar mood he was in. She was right, he'd been careless, which made his mood even darker.

Still, he couldn't just bite her head off, not if she didn't deserve it. That wouldn't be right and he'd made a point of always abiding by what was right, by walking the straight and narrow path even when others veered away from it.

He always had.

Which made that accusation that had ruined his life that much more bitterly ironic.

So he blew out a breath, and with it the words that had sprung to his tongue, if not his lips. Instead, after a beat, Smith grudgingly nodded his head. "You're right. My fault."

Since he'd just admitted it was his mistake and not hers, the anger Jane had felt heat up so quickly within her died back. Leaving her feeling awkward.

She looked up at Smith—he had to be almost a foot taller than she was—a little ruefully, the way she did each time their paths crossed. She remembered him. With his dirty-blond hair, magnetic brown eyes and chiseled good looks, he would have been a hard man to forget.

Smith Parker had been in one of her English classes when she'd attended the university. The one taught by Professor Harrison. Back then, she'd had a bit of a crush on Smith. Maybe more than just a bit. She'd been trying to work up the courage to say something to him, when suddenly, just like that, he was gone.

The rumor was he'd been caught stealing things from one of the girls' dorms, forcing the university to take away his scholarship. She'd heard that his grades dropped right after that. And then he was gone.

Shortly thereafter, she went on to meet and then to marry Drew.

She hadn't thought about Smith in years until one day, not that long ago, she'd seen him hunkered down against a wall in one of the classrooms, working on what appeared to be a faulty outlet.

Standing there that day, looking at him, she couldn't help wondering if he remembered her. But the brown eyes that she recalled as being so vivid had appeared almost dead as they'd turned to look at her. Like two blinds pulled down, barring access to a view she'd once believed was there. There was no recognition to be found when he looked at her.

Or through her, which was how it had felt.

Still, because of the incident in his past, because of the shame that was attached to it, she was never comfortable around Smith. Because she knew about it, it was as if she'd been privy to some dirty, little, dark secret of his. She found pretending not to know him the easier way to go.

She cleared her throat as he stood beside the ladder, looking at her. "Are you all right?"

He half shrugged at the question. "Yeah, thanks to your quick hands."

Something shivered through her as he said that, although she had no idea why. A smattering of those old feelings she'd once secretly harbored about him struggled to the surface.

Jane pushed them back. She wasn't that girl anymore. Wasn't a girl at all, really. A great deal of time had gone by since then and she'd discovered that the world was really a hard, cold, disagreeable place. If it wasn't, then people like the professor could go on about their chosen professions, professions they loved, until they ceased to draw breath.

And if the world wasn't such a disagreeable place, she wouldn't have made such an awful mistake, wouldn't have allowed herself to fall so hard for a student two years ahead of her. Wouldn't have impulsively married him instead of thinking things through.

She shrugged, that same awkward feeling she always felt around Smith returning to claim her. "I've got a five-year-old."

Smith looked at her blankly as he moved the ladder a good foot away from the path of the door. He hadn't really been around any kids since he'd been one himself. The explanation she'd given him created no impression in its wake.

"I don't follow."

She smiled. No, she didn't suppose he did. She'd nosed around a little and discovered that Smith was very much alone these days. No children, no wife, no attachments whatsoever. The world she lived in, even without the constant demand of bills that needed paying, was probably foreign to him.

"Danny is a little hyper." She considered her words, then amended them. "Actually, he's a lot hyper."

Smith moved his head from side to side slowly. "I still don't—"

He *really* didn't know anything about kids, did he? "Okay, let me put it to you this way. Danny never really took his first step. He took his first leap—off a coffee table."

She remembered how her heart had stopped in the middle of her throat. One minute her son had been crawling on the floor beside the table and she'd looked away for a split second. The very next minute he'd clambered up not only to his feet but to the top of the coffee table where he proceeded to take a fearless half-gainer on wobbly, chubby legs while gleefully laughing.

"I was just lucky enough to be there to catch him." She'd all but sprained her ankle getting there in time to keep him from making ignoble contact with the floor. A smile curved her lips as she remembered another incident. All incidents involving Danny fared far better when they were relived than during the original go-round.

"And last year, during the holiday season, I was walking through a department store with Danny, holding his hand. Which left his other hand free to grab the branch of one of the trees they had just finished putting up. He got hold of a string of lights and if my mother's radar hadn't kicked in, the tree would have gone over, flattening another customer." She'd swung around just in time to right the tree. The shoe department manager, whose area it had been, hadn't looked very happy about the matter, despite the smile pasted on his lips.

Smith tried not to notice the way her smile seemed to light up her face. And curl into his system. "Sounds like you have your hands full."

And her life, she thought. "Keeps me on my toes, that's for sure."

He knew she worked full time. Did five-year-olds attend school? He'd never had a reason to know before. He hadn't one now, he reminded himself. This was just conversation and now that he thought of it, he was having it more or less against his will.

Still, he heard himself asking, "Who watches Danny when you're here?"

Kindergarten would be starting for Danny soon. Another hurdle and rite of passage all rolled into one to go through, she mused. But for now, he was still her little boy and she was hanging on to that for as long as possible.

"Some very exhausted day-care center people." The cost of which, she added silently, ate huge chunks out of her weekly paycheck. But it was a good day-care center and Danny seemed to be thriving in the environment, which was all that mattered. She couldn't ask for anything better than that.

Except, maybe, a father for the boy. But that wasn't ever going to happen. For Danny to get a father, she would have to start dating again. Have to put herself out there emotionally again. After the mega-disaster that was her marriage, she had come to the conclusion that she and love had nothing in common.

Unless, of course, she was thinking of love for her son. Or the professor.

Smith caught himself studying Jane. Minding his own business to a fault, he knew very little about the lives of the people around him. He'd never pictured Jane with a son. Hadn't really thought of her as married, either. But that was because she still used the same last name she'd had when they were students in English class together. He'd been aware of her from the first day of class. The cute little redhead with the pale green eyes, soft voice and perfect shape. He'd even come close to asking her out. Back then, he'd thought anything was possible.

But that was before he learned that it wasn't. Not for him.

Smith glanced down at her hand and didn't see a wedding ring. Was she one of those independent women who didn't care for outward signs of commitment? Or hadn't acquiring a husband along with a son been part of her plan?

"Don't you miss him?" he asked.

She wondered if Smith had always been this abrupt or if getting caught and then having to leave the university had done this to him. What was he doing here, anyway? If something that traumatic had happened to her, she certainly wouldn't have come back, asking for a job. She would have starved first.

Maybe that was what he was faced with, she suddenly thought. Compassion flooded through her. "Miss him?" She didn't quite understand what he was driving at. "I see Danny every morning and evening."

Smith shook his head. His own mother had stayed home to raise him, returning to the work force only after he entered middle school. "No, I meant, wouldn't you rather stay home and take care of him?"

A soft smile flirted with the corners of her mouth. "In a perfect world, yes." And then she laughed shortly. The world was so far from perfect, it was staggering. "But if I stayed home, the cupboard would get bare incredibly fast."

"Your husband doesn't work?"

Smith had no idea where that question even came from. For that matter, he didn't even know why he was talking to her. Ordinarily he didn't exchange more than a barely audible grunt with people he passed in the hall. Especially the ones he recognized from his initial years as a student. Those he avoided whenever possible.

Only Professor Harrison was the exception. But that was because the man seemed to insist on taking an interest in him. Long ago, he'd decided that the professor, like his parents, was one of the few good people that were scattered sparingly through the earth.

He noticed that Jane stiffened when he mentioned the word "husband." Obviously he must have hit a nerve.

"I have no idea what my husband does. And he's my ex, actually."

The very thought of Drew brought with it a wealth of silent recriminations. Looking back now, she had no idea why she had been so stupid, not just to put up with his infidelities, which he'd never really made much of an effort to hide, but with his abuse, as well. A self-respecting woman would have never stood for any of that, especially the latter.

Smith saw her jaw harden. Time to back away. He hadn't meant to get into any kind of verbal exchange with Jane, much less wander into personal terrain. In general he'd found that the less he interacted with people, the better he liked it.

He imagined from her tone that she felt the same way, at least in this case. It probably embarrassed her, sharing something so personal with a maintenance man. He doubted very much if she even remembered him. Or would remember him ten minutes from now.

After all, in his present capacity, he was one of the invisible ones. One of the people that others looked right past, or through, without having their presence actually register on any kind of a conscious level. People, like bus drivers, waitresses, hotel workers and gardeners, who were there to serve and make life a little easier for the people who felt themselves above them.

Hell, he'd been guilty of that himself once. Filled with high-powered dreams and drive, he'd seen only his own goals, not the people who toiled around him. Working just the way he did now.

"Sorry," he apologized, his voice monotoned. "Didn't mean to sound like I was prying. None of my business, really."

Because of all the baggage her marriage had created, not the least of which was Drew's vanishing act and with it, her alimony and child support payments, Smith had hit a very raw spot. She hated being reminded that she had been such a fool. And that because of her poor choice, Danny wouldn't be able to have the things that his friends did. Right now, he didn't notice, but soon, he would. And that was all her fault.

"No," she snapped, "it's not."

Embarrassed, afraid that he might say something else, Jane abruptly turned on her heel and hurried down the still-darkened hallway. The sound of her three inch heels clicked against the vinyl until they finally faded out of earshot.

For a second Smith thought of following her and repeating his apology, but then he shrugged to himself. If he did that, he'd risk getting involved, however peripherally. It was the last thing he wanted or needed. Right now, it was hard enough just getting through the day.

Whistling under his breath, he got back up the ladder and finally attended to the bulb that he had originally set out to change.

As Smith began to climb back down, he saw Professor Harrison opening his door very slowly and peering out. Unlike the first time, the door completely cleared the space without coming in contact with the ladder. If Jane hadn't come out like gangbusters, Smith thought, she wouldn't have rocked his ladder and there would have been no need for any kind of verbal exchange to have taken place.

And he wouldn't have noticed how pale and beautiful her eyes still were.

The professor looked up at him, as if startled to see him there. He shifted the files he was carrying to his other side. "Oh, Smith, I almost didn't see you."

"A lot of that happening lately," Smith murmured nearly under his breath.

Gilbert looked up toward the ceiling and saw the new bulb. He shaded his eyes and smiled broadly. "Ah, illumination again. I knew I could count on you, Smith."

The professor made it sound as if he'd just slain a dragon for him, or, at the very least, solved some kind of complicated mathematical equation that had eluded completion up until now.

Smith frowned. "It's just a bulb, professor. No big deal."

The expression on the professor's face said he knew

better. The old man was getting eccentric, Smith thought. The next words out of the man's mouth seemed to underscore his feelings.

"Better to light one candle, Smith, than to curse the dark."

That was probably a quote from somewhere, Smith thought. What it had to do with the situation was beyond him, but he didn't have the time or the inclination to discuss it. He'd had enough conversation for one day. For a week, really.

"Yeah, well, I've got to be going…" Taking the two sides of the ladder, he pulled them together, then tilted it until it was all the way over to the side. It was easier to carry that way, although by no means easy. He silently cursed whoever had taken the extension pole. "I've got another 'candle to light' over on the third floor in the science building."

About to leave, he felt the professor's hand on his arm.

"Something else I can do for you, professor?"

Gilbert looked at the young man for a long moment. There was a time when Smith Parker had been one of his more promising students. He'd been like some bright, burning light, capable of so much. And then, just like that, the light had been extinguished. His pride wounded, Smith had dropped out of Saunders after those charges had been leveled against him, charges he could never get himself to believe were true. But Smith had left before he'd had the chance to try to talk to him, to see about making things right again.

"Smith, have you given any thought to your future?"

It wasn't what he'd expected the professor to say.

And it certainly wasn't anything that he wanted to get into a discussion about. "Yeah, I have. Right after I replace the other bulb, I'm having lunch," Smith replied crisply. "Now, if you'll excuse me."

The professor dropped his hand from Smith's arm.

Before there could be any further conversation, Smith hefted the ladder beneath his arm and made his way down the hall.

Chapter Three

Just as Smith managed to clear the corner without hitting anything with the unwieldy ladder, he realized that he'd left behind the box of light bulbs. Most likely, it was still on the floor in the hall next to Professor Harrison's office.

Stifling a curse born of an impatience he couldn't quite seem to put a lid on today, Smith put the ladder down, leaning it against the wall as best as possible. He was pretty certain that no one would walk into it where it was. Even if the school year were under way now, this area of the building saw very little foot traffic.

Smith paused to wipe the sweat from his brow, stuffed his handkerchief into his back pocket and doubled back to the professor's office. Just as he walked into that part of the hallway, he stopped in his tracks.

The professor was across the hall from his office and juxtaposed to Jane's. He was unlocking the door to a storage room that was tucked between the door that led to the stairwell and east wall of the building. It was a room that saw, as far as Smith knew, next to no activity at all. For all intents and purposes, it was a forgotten room, an appendage no one paid any attention to. He hadn't even been given a key to the room when Thom Dolan, the head of the maintenance department, had given him the sets for all the buildings that had been assigned to his care.

"Nobody ever uses that room," Dolan had informed him on the first day while giving him a tour of the building. The heavyset man had lowered his voice before continuing, as if what he was about to say was a dark secret. But then, he'd noted that Dolan was given to drama. "Rumor has it that this place was built on the site of a boys' reformatory. This was one of the original buildings. During that time, the people who ran this place used to stick the kids who gave them the most trouble into that room. It's small, boxlike, with no windows. As far as I know, there's only junk being stored in there now. No need for you to have a key to it. Hell, I'm not even sure there is a key for that room."

Well, the professor obviously had a key to it, Smith thought now. He had no idea what prompted him to step back and keep his presence from being detected. Granted, by nature, he was no longer the type to call out a greeting when encountering someone he knew. That had been the teenager, not the man. Besides, he and the professor had just spoken. If he called out to him, the professor would undoubtedly pick up where he'd left off, asking about his "future." There was no such animal and he had no desire to discuss it.

Still, stepping back so that he wasn't readily seen by the professor made him feel as if he were skulking. That didn't exactly sit well with him.

But there was just something almost suspicious, for lack of a better word, Smith thought, about the professor's behavior right now. Before putting the key into the lock, the older man had looked over his shoulder toward Jane's office, as if to make sure that the door was still closed and that no one saw him.

Why?

Smith thought for a moment, waiting for the professor to go into the room.

Maybe the old man was losing it. Maybe all those long hours he'd kept, sitting in his office amid dust that was never quite removed, just regularly disturbed by halfhearted attempts on the part of the cleaning crew to live up to its name. Baskets were emptied regularly and what could be seen of the worn beige carpet between the stacks of files and books haphazardly scattered around the professor's office was vacuumed on a weekly basis, but the dust remained as permanent a resident as the books on the shelves.

That kind of thing had to eventually affect a man's lungs, Smith decided. And who was to say that what the professor had breathed in hadn't finally left its mark on the man's mind, as well?

Still, the professor did seem to be more or less all right whenever they did run into each other. Harrison always had a good word for him, whether he wanted to hear it or not. When you came right down to it, of all the people on the faculty, only Professor Harrison seemed to see him, to treat him as a person rather than a tool or a lackey to be told what to do and then disregarded. Granted, the man had become a great deal sadder in these last eight months than he'd normally been, but he hadn't withdrawn from life, hadn't used it as an excuse to be curt or mean in his dealings.

For a second Smith debated saying something to let the professor know that he wasn't alone in the hallway. He did feel somewhat deceptive about standing in the shadows like this.

But then he decided that none of this was really any of his business and the professor obviously wanted whatever he was doing to be kept secret. Otherwise, he wouldn't have looked around so furtively before unlocking the door.

So he waited until the professor disappeared inside the room before moving out into the hallway. Picking up the box of light bulbs he'd returned for in the first place, Smith walked away before the professor emerged out of the room.

For the first time in a long while, Smith found that his curiosity had been aroused. He figured a stiff drink or two after work this evening would effectively take care of that.

The Sandwich Bar had been more crowded than Jane had anticipated today. A lot of the returning students were on campus to purchase new books for the coming semester, or just to settle back into their dorms in anti-cipation of the routine that was to come. A quick ten-minute venture had turned into half an hour.

She hurried to the professor's office and dropped his order on his desk. He wasn't around, but she assumed that he'd just stepped out for the moment and would be back shortly. Leaving his office, she hurried across the hall to her own.

Lunchtime was more than half over. Not that the pro-fessor ever placed any boundaries on her time. More than once he'd told her she could take as long as she wanted for lunch in case there were any errands she needed to run. He'd said that he knew a single mother with a young son had demands on her time that couldn't always be neatly tucked away within the hours that came after she left the college for the evening.

But the university had a strict policy as to how long anyone could take for lunch and she didn't want to be seen abusing it. It was bad enough that the board was after the professor. She didn't want them saying that his secretary was found wanting, as well, and in some twisted way use that against him, too.

So she was going to have her lunch at her desk while she caught up on some data she needed to input into her computer. God knew she was behind this week. She'd taken the last week off, wanting to spend some time with Danny before he took that first big step into the world of learning. From here on in, once school began for him, her son's next seventeen years plus were going to be accounted for.

She thought of that time in terms of money and the

very notion sent a long, cold shiver shimmying down her spine.

Somewhere, somehow, she was going to find the money for Danny's college education. There would be no mysterious benefactors for her son the way there had been for her, but that didn't mean he was going to be deprived. Danny was going to receive his college diploma even if she had to work 24/7 to get the money.

Jane stopped her train of thought. There were times, she knew, when she got a little too carried away.

"First, you need to let Danny get through kindergarten," she told herself as she opened the door to her cramped office.

Jane stopped in the doorway. There was a tall, slender blonde standing in her office with her back to the door, taking up what felt like one quarter of the tiny space.

"Can I help you?"

The woman turned around. Jane felt a little foolish, thinking that this was a stranger. Not that they were exactly friends, but they knew one another. They'd both been at Saunders the same year and had had some classes together. Their lives, however, had gone on to take completely different paths.

For some reason Sandra was in her office, obviously waiting for her. Jane tried to think if there was anything remotely newsworthy going on. Sandra was a journalist for a neighborhood newspaper in Boston's North End, given to writing human interest stories and short, entertaining articles about up-coming local functions. Sandra was also the wife of one-time Saunders University jock, David Westport. Jane remembered that the two had been college sweethearts around the same time that she and Drew had gotten together. Theirs was a match thought to be made in heaven, or at least a successful Hollywood romance movie.

Nice to know some marriages actually worked, Jane thought.

Still looking at Sandra, she put down the bag with her sandwich and her tall container of soda, the caffeine in which she hoped would see her through the long afternoon. Danny'd had nightmares last night. Twice. The second time he'd come running into her room, she'd taken him back to his and then stayed up with him until long past when he'd settled back to sleep. She estimated that since Danny had been born, she'd averaged roughly five hours of sleep a night—if she was lucky.

Without a doubt, she was going to need more than one hit of caffeine. *After* she found out what the ex-cheerleader was doing here.

Sandra moved away from the window she'd been looking out of. "I certainly hope you can help."

Jane's eyebrows pulled together thoughtfully. She had absolutely no idea what she could possibly do to help someone like Sandra. At first glance—and twelfth—Sandra seemed to have it all: beauty, a job she liked and, most important of all, a loving husband.

But Jane was nothing if not game. Sticking a straw through the small hole in the soda container's lid, she took a long, refreshing sip, then looked up at the other woman in the room.

"Okay, I'm listening."

"Please, go ahead and have your lunch," Sandra told

her, waving at the brown bag with its whimsical logo of a college student devouring a three-foot sandwich. "I promise this won't take too long."

Now Sandra really had her intrigued. Despite the fact that marriage to Drew had made her always expect the worst, no matter what the turn of events, Jane was struggling hard to break that habit.

But it wasn't easy. Especially when Sandra's pretty heart-shaped face looked so tense, despite the smile she'd so obviously forced to her lips.

"And 'this' would be?" Jane prompted, taking out her sandwich.

Sandra sank onto the chair that was directly against the side of the desk and looked at Jane. "I'm sure by now you know that the board is trying to get rid of Professor Harrison."

Jane wasn't thrilled with Sandra's imperious tone. "Yes, I'm aware of what's happening," she said coolly. She waited for Sandra to continue.

Sandra flushed. "Sorry. I didn't mean to sound as if I've got some kind of inside track. If anyone does, it's you. Which is why I'm here." She took a breath, then launched into the heart of the matter. "The professor called on a few people—David, Nate Williams and a couple of others—asking them to come and speak to the board on his behalf." Sandra's mouth curved into a smile that seemed to Jane to be more sad than happy. "I guess he thought if he could show off some of his success stories, they wouldn't come down so hard on his 'old-fashioned' methods."

Jane was well aware of the professor's plan. He'd had

her scan the Internet for phone numbers of a handful of his former students who had gone on to make something of themselves so that he could get in touch with them.

She'd noted that although she and the professor were close and she worked with him every day, the professor hadn't asked *her* to address the board on his behalf. She supposed he might have thought it was putting her on the spot. Nothing could have been further from the truth. She had every intention of speaking up for him.

Granted she wasn't a shining example of what one could achieve given the advantages of an education at Saunders and the benefit of having sat in one of Professor Harrison's classes. But it didn't matter that her personal life was in a state of flux and upheaval. That was certainly no fault of the professor's. After her parents' death, if it hadn't been for the professor, she wouldn't have found the courage to complete her education. Coupled with the mysterious bequest that had taken the financial burden off her shoulders, she'd been able to graduate and receive her diploma. But she wouldn't have been able to do it on just money alone. The state of her emotions had been an equal if not more important factor in her attaining her diploma. The professor had helped her to believe in herself.

She wasn't sure just how much of an impact she would have, pleading the professor's case. After all, she wasn't some high-powered doctor, or famous lawyer, or internationally known model like the people he'd contacted. She was just an administrative assistant, which in her case was a glorified euphemism for secretary.

Still, that didn't take away from the fact that Professor Harrison had left a tremendous, lasting impression on her life, one for which she would be forever grateful. To her way of thinking, he should be allowed to do the same for the students of the classes that were to come.

Jane nodded in response to Sandra's words. "That sounds just like the way the professor thinks," she agreed.

Eager to get started, Sandra continued, "I've discovered that Alex Broadstreet intends to humiliate the professor, to twist things around and accuse him of improper behavior."

Jane looked at her, stunned. She'd almost dropped the sandwich she was unwrapping. Of all the absurd things she'd ever heard in her life, this had to take the prize. "Improper behavior? That's ridiculous. Professor Harrison is the epitome of a gentleman. He's—"

Sandra held up her hand, realizing the confusion. "No, I don't mean harassment. Improper things like grade tampering."

Jane's eyes widened. "Cheating? He's going to accuse the professor of cheating? To what end?"

Sandra shrugged helplessly. "I don't know. Maybe for money?"

Jane felt as if she'd been insulted herself. Indignation for the professor's honor swelled in her chest. "That is the most mean-spirited, awful thing I have ever, *ever* heard—"

"I totally agree," Sandra quickly interrupted. She shook her head at the half sandwich Jane offered her. "Thanks, but I already ate." She blew out a breath, addressing the reason she was here. "But protesting how heinous the accusation is isn't enough. By all accounts, Alex Broadstreet is a very, very clever man. He wants to bring Saunders University into the twenty-first century, to shed the 'quaint' aura and turn Saunders into a college that all the moneyed captains of industry want their children to attend. The professor isn't fast-tracked enough for him, so he has to go. And Broadstreet undoubtedly feels he's just the man to make him do that."

Broadstreet could "feel" that all he wanted to, but that still didn't change the fact that Gilbert Harrison was the most principled man June had ever met. "I still don't see how—"

Sandra smiled at her. Whether the journalist was aware of it or not, she was also guilty of delivering a slight, almost-derogatory shake of the head, as well, as if to say that Sandra thought her to be naive. She might be a lot of things, Jane thought, but naive was no longer one of them. Not after Drew.

She raised her chin defensively as her eyes narrowed. "He can't do anything honestly."

Sandra laughed shortly. "I don't think Broadstreet troubles himself with things like strict honesty. It's all in the phrasing."

"Phrasing?"

"You know," Sandra urged, "It's like saying, 'So when did you stop beating your wife, Professor Harrison?' When the person protests that he didn't stop, it doesn't really matter that he didn't stop because he'd never started, the implication that he beat his wife is there, in the mind of the listener. The seed has been planted. And Broadstreet will be the first with a shovel in his hand to add some nice, warm dirt so that it can thrive." She looked at Jane pointedly. "We need to make sure that there isn't any 'dirt' he can use." Sandra relaxed a little, now that she'd gotten rolling. "In addition, there's that urban legend—"

She really needed to get more sleep, Jane thought. She was having trouble following Sandra as the former cheerleader leaped from one thing to another. "Legend? What legend?"

"You know." Everyone in their graduating class had heard talk about it. About one of their own being on the receiving end of some scholarship or bequest of money that no one had ever heard about before. "About the mysterious benefactor." Since Jane said nothing, Sandra continued to elaborate. "Money that suddenly appears to help a financially strapped student—" She stopped abruptly when she saw Jane's face go pale. "What's the matter?"

Jane had never really paid much attention to rumors and campus gossip about the so-called benefactor who anonymously gave all kinds of aid to students in need. When the money had first turned up, she'd made a few attempts to track down the source of her sudden windfall, but quickly came to a dead end each time. She'd finally just come to think of it as her own personal miracle. No one she knew had that kind of money to lavish on a newly orphaned student and there was no family, however far flung, to have come to her rescue. That qualified it as a miracle.

Until now.

"It's not a legend," she told Sandra. "I had money

placed into an account for me when I was attending Saunders."

Sandra stared at her. The reporter in her was making copious mental notes. "It just suddenly appeared one day?"

Hearing Sandra say it, it sounded almost ludicrously unbelievable. But truth had a way of being stranger than fiction.

"Basically, yes. There was a letter saying the money was to pay for the remainder of my tuition. Whatever was left over was to be used for housing and books. I got a job waiting tables off campus and the earnings plus the 'gift' was enough for me to stay on at Saunders and get my diploma."

Sandra could barely contain her excitement. Maybe they could show that the professor somehow had a hand in this, maybe through quietly soliciting donations from charitable foundations for deserving students. The wheels in her head began whirling.

First things first, she warned herself. "Who was the letter from?"

"The administrative office." Jane could still recall how stunned she'd been, opening the letter and holding it in her hands. She'd thought she was dreaming. She remembered weeping for a long time.

Sandra leaped to the logical conclusion. "So it was a school scholarship—"

But Jane shook her head. "No, that's just it. It wasn't. Not the way the letter was worded."

Sandra looked at her intently, as if willing her to have total recollection of the event. "And just how was it worded? Exactly."

Sandra was asking more of her than she could give. Again, Jane shook her head.

"I can't remember." And then, to prevent the other woman from thinking that she was some kind of an airhead, she explained, "You have to understand, my parents had just been killed in a car accident. I was all alone in the world and I wasn't exactly thinking clearly about anything. When the letter came, it was like the answer to a prayer. I couldn't believe it. If that money hadn't come when it had, I would have had to drop out of school."

The way Smith had.

The thought brought her up short. Where had that come from?

And why?

With renewed verve, Jane pushed on, her sandwich completely forgotten. "All my parents had was a small insurance policy that would have barely taken care of burial expenses. Eventually, I had to sell our house to pay off most of their other bills."

It had been a point of honor with her, even though Drew had called her a fool for doing it when she'd told him what she had done. She didn't add that her father had had a problem hanging on to money. That he spent it faster than he earned it, striving for a lifestyle he couldn't afford. No one, except the professor, knew about that. Not even Drew. Though her mother had loved her father, they'd argued a great deal about his compulsion.

There was no doubt in her mind that her parents were probably arguing about it the day they were killed. The driver of the semi that hit their car swore that the driver looked as if he'd had his face turned away from the road.

Sandra digested the information, trying to turn it to their best advantage. "Do you think there's a chance that the professor might have had something to do with your windfall?"

Not likely, Jane thought. The salary of a college professor was far from a king's ransom. Certainly not enough to secretly bestow the kind of money it took to attend Saunders on a number of students. Or even one student for that matter.

"I sincerely doubt it. When I worked in the administration building in the accounts office, I got to see what Professor Harrison, along with the rest of the staff, earned. Not nearly enough money to play fairy godmother. Why?"

Sandra shrugged. "I'm looking for something, anything, that might put him in the very best possible light in front of the board. If we could somehow show that Professor Harrison gathered together funds from other sources to help needy—" she quickly substituted another word and hoped that Jane didn't notice "—um, deserving students, then maybe…"

That wasn't the way to go, Jane thought. "I'm sure he would have said something to me in all this time if he was involved in some kind of charitable action." Her eyes met Sandra's. "We can't lie to the board about that, tempting as it might be. Somehow, Broadstreet would call us on it."

Sandra sighed. It had been a nice idea while it lasted—all of six seconds. "I know."

Jane took another long sip of her soda, then asked, "So, what is it you'd like me to do?"

This time, Sandra proceeded slowly, building word on word. "You said you used to work in the administration building, right?"

That was a matter of record. It was a job she knew the professor'd had a hand in getting for her, just as he'd gotten her this one when his own secretary had retired. "Yes."

"All the old files are archived in the basement." Sandra didn't wait for Jane to confirm the fact. "Maybe if we go through the ones pertaining to the professor's former students and the others he advised, we can find something that we can use. I really don't know what we're looking for until we find it," she confessed. "But I do think it's worth a try. And I do need your help." Sandra looked at her hopefully. "Can I count on it?"

"I'll do anything to help the professor," Jane told her. "That goes without saying."

"Wonderful." Sandra took her hand in both of hers and shook it heartily. "I'll get back to you on this. Soon," she promised.

Walking out quickly, Sandra left Jane pondering the situation. Chewing on a sandwich she didn't taste, Jane wondered if there was anything else she could do to help further the professor's cause. She felt energized and at the same time at a loss as to where to place all that energy.

She supposed she didn't have to wait for Sandra's go-ahead. She could just get started doing what the woman had suggested. Looking.

Except there was one thing wrong with that.

Sandra's basic supposition had been flawed, Jane thought. She knew where the files were kept, all right, but she couldn't get at them. They were in the basement, under lock and key. To get to look at them, she was going to need to unlock the door to the room where they were all archived.

Which meant she needed a key. Either that or a handy burglar.

She couldn't ask anyone in the administration office to unlock the door. They'd want to know what she was doing. Most likely, they'd want to go down to the basement with her. She couldn't very well say she was hunting for documentation showing what an excellent man and educator the professor was. Word undoubtedly would get back to Broadstreet and then they really wouldn't be able to get at the files. There was no telling if someone in the administration office was trying to curry favor with Broadstreet. She had a feeling the man had spies everywhere.

What she needed, Jane thought, was to approach someone she felt confident was in no one's pocket. Someone who would never run and tell Broadstreet or the board what she was up to.

Outside, it was beginning to rain. Within a blink of an eye, her office was cast into shadow, turning afternoon into practically night.

She reached across her desk and turned on the lamp. As light filled the room, Jane smiled to herself.

There was someone she could ask. Someone, she instinctively knew, who was in no one's pocket and never would be.

Chapter Four

Some twenty minutes after she'd put in a call to Thom Dolan in the maintenance department, requesting that he send Smith Parker up to her office, there was a quick, sharp rap on her door.

Before she could say, "Come in," he did.

Looking, Jane thought, not unlike a thundercloud casting ominous shadows over the western plains. There were even some drops of rain clinging to his hair, as the rain had just let up.

It was obvious that Smith didn't care for being summoned, but that couldn't be helped. She didn't have the luxury of waiting until their paths crossed again, especially since they did so seldomly.

Smith moved closer to her desk, his very presence

making the room feel even smaller than it was. The man had muscles, she thought absently.

"What's the emergency?" he all but growled.

Without intending to, she pushed her chair back a little. "No emergency," Jane answered. "I just needed to talk to you."

Wheat-colored eyebrows pulled together over the bridge of his finely shaped nose. Smith looked at her very skeptically, as if waiting for a punch line. "You called me in here to talk?"

Now that Smith was actually here, she wasn't sure just how to proceed, how to phrase her request. Except for today outside the professor's office, whenever they did run into one another, the most she'd say was hello because she didn't know whether or not he wanted her to acknowledge the fact that they knew one another.

When she'd first seen him wearing the navy-blue jumpsuit with the university's logo across the back and the title of Maintenance Engineer finely stitched across his breast pocket, she had been completely dumbstruck. She remembered thinking that there had to be some mistake, or maybe even some kind of a joke. Either that, or the maintenance man was a dead ringer for the student who had sat two rows away from her. They couldn't possibly be one and the same.

The Smith Parker she was acquainted with had been very bright. When he'd abruptly left Saunders shortly after those accusations had been brought against him, she'd just assumed that Smith had gone on to attend another college. And a man with a college degree didn't concern himself with clogged pipes unless they were in his own house.

But then she'd heard him say something to one of the teachers and she knew it had to be Smith. His voice, low in timbre, sensual even if he were merely reciting the alphabet, was unmistakable. With every syllable he uttered, his voice seemed to undulate right under her skin.

Just the way it seemed to do now.

Feeling suddenly nervous, Jane cleared her throat. "Actually, I wanted to see you because I need a favor from you."

Smith put down the toolbox he'd brought with him and looked at her as if she was speaking in riddles.

"A favor," he echoed slowly, taking the word apart letter by letter, as if that would reveal something beneath it. When she nodded and he was no closer to an answer than before, Smith prodded, "What kind of favor?"

As he asked, he glanced around the office. The size of a broom closet on steroids, it still managed to be cheery because of the few personal touches she had added to it. On the wall directly behind her was a poster of a kitten, its front paws wrapped around a tree branch as its back legs dangled in midair. The animal looked precariously close to falling. For some reason that eluded him, the kitten made him think of her.

Beneath it, in white script, was the slogan "Hang in There." He wondered how many times a day Jane said that to herself. Subconsciously he'd been saying something along those lines to himself for some time now. Of late, he'd had this feeling that something better was going to be coming his way if he was just patient enough to wait it out.

He guessed that maybe his spirit wasn't entirely dead the way he'd once believed it to be.

Aside from the poster, Jane had left the walls unadorned. Looking at them now, he could see that they could stand a fresh coat of paint.

He made a judgment call as to the nature of her as yet unspoken request. "Would that favor have anything to do with giving this room a makeover?"

About to cautiously put her case before him, Smith's words threw her. She looked at him quizzically. Where would he have gotten that idea from? She'd never complained to anyone about her office. After being part of a large collective over in the administration building, she valued this little bit of turf that was her own—for as long as she had her job.

"Excuse me?"

Confusion made her look adorable.

The observation had slipped in out of nowhere, surprising him. Smith sent it packing back to the same place.

Waving his hand around the space around him, he elaborated, "The room, it could stand a paint job. Is that the reason you sent for me?" he asked, enunciating each word slowly because she looked as if he'd lapsed into a foreign tongue.

Jane could almost feel every single word moving along her body before it faded away.

Nerves, just nerves, she told herself. She wasn't accustomed to asking for favors, even if it wasn't for herself. It made her uncomfortable.

But this wasn't about her, Jane reminded herself. It was about the professor. Who had been there for her when she'd needed someone.

She shook her head dismissively. "Maybe someday, but no, that wasn't what I meant."

Smith didn't appear to hear her. His attention had obviously wandered and so had he. Over to the weeping fig tree she'd bought a month ago. It had been on sale, standing in front of a local florist shop. Passing it, the tree had caught her eye and she could envision it brightening up the dark corner of her office. Ficus benjamina was its botanical name. She called it "Benny" for short.

Right now, tall, thin and pale, Benny looked as if he needed to be placed on a respirator. His grasp on life appeared a little tenuous.

Smith touched one of the wispy branches. Two leaves immediately fell off. It felt as if he'd just raised the limb of a terminal patient. Why did people buy plants only to neglect them? he wondered.

He looked at her over his shoulder. "You're killing this, you know."

God, he was a strange man. "No, I'm not," she retorted defensively. "Benny's just adjusting to his surroundings."

"Benny?" He raised his head and looked at her just as she'd rounded her desk and walked over to him. She was wearing a skirt whose hem was even with the tips of her fingers when her hands were at her sides. He tried not to stare at her legs.

"That's what I call him. And I'm not killing him," she repeated.

He loved plants, had an affinity for them, but he'd

never named one. That she did seemed more than a little odd to him.

"Yes," he replied firmly, "you are." Stooping, he took the side of the wicker pot she'd placed the fig tree in and slowly turned it around. The slight movement caused more leaves to come raining down. There were less than two dozen left on the sapling. "It's not supposed to look like Greta Garbo in *Camille*."

She bent beside him, completely lost. "Who?"

Feeling suddenly hemmed in by her presence, Smith rose to his feet. "Greta Garbo." Her face remained blank and he shrugged. "Never mind." It didn't matter if Jane didn't understand his comparison. What did matter, though, was that the plant was dying. And it didn't have to be. "The point is, this plant is going to die unless you do something."

She'd followed the instructions on the little card that had been attached to one of its branches. There hadn't been many, but the shop owner had assured her that the tree was hardy and once it adjusted to its new surroundings, it would thrive.

She fisted her hands on her hips. "Like what?"

Because of its location, the room saw very little sun, getting its illumination, instead, from the overhead lighting. He pointed toward the lone window in the office, even though it was still overcast outside.

"Give it sun, fresh air, a chance to breathe, introduce vitamins into its water, get some fertilizer for it." It might not be too late, he judged, studying the plant's pale color. Here and there were a few new green shoots

trying to push through. "Otherwise, its chances of surviving are next to none."

She had no idea having a plant was so complicated.
To her, plants were to be watered and, for the most part,
ignored. "You sound like a doctor talking about a patient in the E.R."

"Plants are living things and should be accorded respect." Putting his finger into the soil, he found it was
bone-dry. Smith saw the large empty soda container
she'd thrown out. Taking it from the wastebasket, he
walked out without saying another word, leaving her
flabbergasted. But he was back in a few minutes, the cup
now filled with water. He poured the contents into the
pot. "This should be outdoors."

He made it sound like an accusation. And that she
had broken some cardinal rule. Jane bristled before she
could rein herself in. "It's an indoor tree."

The look he gave her all but asked if she believed in
the tooth fairy, as well. "There's no such thing as an indoor tree, unless it's a treehouse and you happen to be
Tarzan. That's just a ploy to help sell this to people with
no gardens."

She decided to do an about-face and put the ball in
his court. "Okay, since you know so much, can you
'save' Benny for me, Smith?"

He looked at her sharply. Not because of what she'd
asked him to do, but because she'd used his name. It was
the first time he'd heard her say it. Since she hadn't said
anything up to this point, he'd just assumed she hadn't
recognized him.

"You know my name?"

Jane stared at him incredulously for a second. "Of course I know your name. How do you think I asked for you?"

For a second he'd forgotten that she'd put in a request for him. They'd come almost full circle. Smith glanced down at his uniform. His name was supposed to be embroidered over his pocket, just beneath the politically correct jog title. Wanting to be as anonymous as possible, he'd opted to leave the space blank.

"I'll bite. How?"

Something inside her began to falter again. Life with Drew had sapped her of her self-esteem and made her doubt her every move. It took effort to conquer her uncertainty, but she had a feeling that Smith didn't suffer cowards well.

It gave them something in common. Neither did she. Especially when that coward was her.

"You were in my English class." And then, even as she said it, another more personal memory came back to her. "You were also the guy who collided with me on the steps of the library that time, knocking all my books out of my arms."

He remembered that. Vividly. Remembered how soft she'd felt against him, despite the momentary collision. Remembered catching her in his arms before she fell. The books had gone flying, but she hadn't. It had taken him a second longer to release her than it should have.

"Yeah, it was raining." His eyes met hers. "And the pages got all wet."

"Not all of them," she allowed, a soft smile taking possession of her mouth.

The incident, during midterm week, had occurred shortly before he'd abruptly dropped out of sight.

Something very personal, almost tangible, hung between them for a moment, making time stand still.

But there was something larger than her own insignificant feelings at stake here. There was the professor to think of. She blew out a breath, searching for the right way to begin again.

Smith was still looking at her, making her skin feel as if it was alive. "I didn't think you recognized me."

She drew conclusions from his tone. "But you recognized me?"

What could have passed as a small smile faintly graced his lips. "Hard not to. You haven't changed much."

That wasn't strictly true, he decided silently. She had. The pretty girl she'd been had blossomed and matured into a woman who was more than lovely. A woman with a subtle beauty that easily turned a man's head when she passed by.

But saying so might give her the wrong idea. Might make her think he thought things he didn't. He just noticed things, that was all. He always had.

She laughed softly at the notion that she hadn't changed. "A lot you know."

It was a leading line and it succeeded in momentarily pulling him in. "Excuse me?"

But she shook her head. She wasn't about to go into anything remotely personal. It made her feel too exposed. Not to mention that she wasn't very proud of the years that had just gone by. She should have never allowed them to happen, never allowed Drew to be as abusive as he had been. Someone with a spine would have walked out a long time ago. He'd even deprived her of that, of the dignity of leaving, because just when she'd made up her mind to leave him, he'd left her.

It seemed that every way she turned, Drew kept robbing her of her dignity.

"Nothing." Jane looked at the weeping fig. Smith was right. The poor thing did look as if it needed some kind of divine intervention. Or, barring that, help from someone who knew what they were doing. That obviously left her out. "I guess I thought it was supposed to look like that."

Smith brushed his fingers along the top layer of dropped leaves inside the pot and grabbed a fistful. The drier ones crackled as he closed his hand over them. He looked at Jane pointedly as he held them up for her benefit.

"Did you think it was supposed to lose this many leaves, too?"

She gave a half shrug. "I'm not very good with plants."

He tossed the leaves into the wastebasket. "Obviously."

She would have taken offense if it wasn't so true. Now that she thought about it, she didn't know what had possessed her to buy Benny in the first place. It was just that it had looked so sad, just standing there outside the store, like a puppy no one wanted to take home.

"Actually," she admitted, "I guess I've got pretty much of a brown thumb. Any living thing I touch, I kill. I'm lucky Danny's still alive." Smith looked at her sharply, as if she'd just confessed to something awful. "It was a joke, Smith."

"Very funny." His retort was dry, flat. She didn't know if he was deadpanning or just being dismissive.

Jane shook her head. "You really need to loosen up a little."

He wasn't in the market for advice and resented the fact that someone who had such a blatant disregard for the care and nurturing of living things felt as if she could offer it.

"Why?"

He was challenging her, she realized, and she said the first thing that came into her head without benefit of censoring it. "Because greeting life with clenched teeth can make your jaw ache after a while."

"Yeah, right." He turned his attention back to things he understood. Like saving the plant. "So, you want me to see what I can do for this thing, or do you just want to watch it die?"

She couldn't make up her mind if he was trying to insult her or if he wasn't aware of the way he came across. This certainly wasn't the guy she'd had a crush on all those years ago. But then, she'd learned that when put to the test, men weren't exactly sterling examples of humanity.

"You certainly do have a way with words." Jane gestured toward the plant. "Be my guest." But as he stooped to wrap his arm around the base of the wicker-framed pot, she stopped him. She didn't want him leaving just yet. Somehow she'd allowed him to sidetrack her. "But that isn't why I asked you to come here."

Rising to his feet, he looked down at her. It took effort not to feel dwarfed or intimidated by him.

"We're not through talking?" Smith wanted to know.

Gracious was not a word in his vocabulary. "Don't make it sound as if I'm forcing cod liver oil down your throat." It was his turn to look at her quizzically. Admittedly, she allowed, the reference had come out of left field. As had the memory. "My mother was a health food nut. Her mother used to give her a spoonful of cod liver oil as a kid to 'keep her healthy,' so she continued the tradition." And, God, had she hated it. Even now she could remember the taste. It had been thick and oily tasting and so hard to swallow.

"It comes in capsules now."

Her mouth curved. The man was a font of strange information. "Good to know." She ran the tip of her tongue along her lips. There was no way to tackle this but head-on, she thought, before another diversion came up and she lost her nerve completely. "Saving my dying tree isn't the favor I was going to ask."

That he could now readily believe. She didn't even seem to realize that her tree was in need of help until he'd pointed it out. He braced himself. "Okay, then what was?"

"Do you have the keys to the basement in the administration building?"

She watched in fascination as suspicion instantly rose in his eyes. This was a man who didn't trust easily. For the first time she found herself really wondering about Smith, about the paths that he had taken to bring him to this point in time. At the very least, she could have pictured him running a maintenance company, not just working for one. Just what had happened to him?

"Why?" Smith asked her.

"Because I need to get in there, specifically into the room where all the old student and administrative files are archived."

Forgetting about the plant that so sorely needed his help, he crossed his arms in front of him and looked at Jane. Her request was unusual to say the least. Her responsibilities now had nothing do with old files, of that much he was certain.

"Why don't you just ask someone in Administration for the key?"

She shook her head. "This isn't something I can ask someone there."

The suspicion in his eyes intensified as he regarded her for a long moment. "But you're asking me."

The why was silent, but there nonetheless. "Because I think I can trust you."

This time he said it out loud. "Why?"

Jane blew out a breath. In a way, it was like trying to reason with Danny. He was always challenging every word out of her mouth, too. But in his case, her very precocious son just wanted to learn. She had no idea why Smith felt compelled to toss the word at her at every turn.

"You know," she said, "you really should have that word painted on a T-shirt for you. It would save time. You could just point to it every time you wanted to say why."

"I'll look into it later. Why?" Smith repeated, his eyes pinning her.

For a second Jane almost felt like squirming. It occurred to her that Smith Parker would have made one hell of a good police interrogator, or for that matter, a lawyer grilling a witness on the stand. Why wasn't he one? She knew for a fact that he had the intelligence for either vocation. Before his abrupt downward spiral, Smith had been getting *A*s in the class they'd taken together. She'd heard most of his academic career had mirrored that.

Jane squared her shoulders. "I need to look into them for the professor. Professor Harrison," she clarified in case he wasn't following her.

God, but he had the most intense brown eyes. They seemed to be staring right through her. Right *into* her, she amended. It took effort not to shift beneath his gaze.

Something wasn't clicking, Smith thought. "He's asking you to do this?"

"No," she said quickly, afraid that Smith just might walk out of here and straight into the professor's office to tell him what she'd just said.

She didn't want the professor to know about this, not yet, anyway. Being honorable, the professor might tell her that she couldn't go into the files without the proper authorization.

Sometimes, she thought, when the cause was right, rules needed to be bent.

"No, he's not. I—we," she amended, "are hoping to find something in the old student files that might help the professor keep his job." She didn't add that she was also going to keep her eye out for anything that might be thought of as damning, as well. To help the professor, they needed to be prepared for all contingencies.

"'We,'" he said slowly, looking at her so intently she

thought she was going to break out in a warm sweat, "as in, you and me?"

"As in me and someone else," she corrected, hoping her voice didn't sound as breathless to him as it did to her. "It doesn't matter who," she added when he looked as if he was going to ask.

It mattered to him. He never entered into anything where he didn't know all parties involved. It was like that adage that said never enter a room or a building where you don't already know how to find the exits. It was the unknown that could trip you up every time. And life had enough potholes as it was.

She was losing him, Jane thought—if she'd ever remotely even had him on her side. An edgy feeling began to scramble up her insides. She pressed on, talking more quickly. "Broadstreet is trying to get rid of the professor."

At the mention of the other man, Smith frowned. Alexander Broadstreet was one of those people who treated everyone as if they were beneath him. There was no love lost between him and the older man. For one thing, Broadstreet reminded him of an older version of Jacob Weber, the student directly to blame for his present lifestyle.

"Yeah, I heard."

Her eyes widened as she stared at him. "And it doesn't gall you?"

"Lots of things 'gall' me, Jane. But that doesn't mean that I'm about to do anything illegal about it."

Was it her imagination or had Smith just placed emphasis on the word "illegal"? Had she offended him somehow? Drudged up bad memories? God, the man was harder to read than the professor's handwriting. "So then your answer is no?"

Smith stooped beside the pot again, picked it up with one arm wrapped around its base. As he stood, he spared her a fleeting look before confirming her assumption. "My answer is no."

Stopping only long enough to pick up his toolbox, Smith walked out the door.

Chapter Five

For a second, Jane leaned against her desk, feeling the sting of disappointment as she wondered if there was any other way she could gain access to the archived files in the basement of the administration building without enlisting the aid of a superhero to get her into the room.

But there wasn't. Smith was her only in.

Which meant she had to find a way to change his mind. Given the look on his face just now as he'd walked out, it wasn't going to be easy. But then, what was?

Pushing away from the desk, Jane rushed out of her office within seconds of his departure.

She hurried into the hallway just in time to see Smith and her ailing fig tree about to round the corner. Glancing toward the door on the other side, she saw that it was closed. There was no light pooling from beneath the door. That meant that the professor was probably still out. Good.

Jane played a hunch and hoped she was right. Raising her voice, she called after Smith. "Did the professor ever help you?"

Smith stopped dead.

How had she known about that?

There was no blatant accusation in her voice, but it was there just the same. Hidden but implied. He knew what Jane was saying. That Professor Harrison had gone out on a limb for him. And now that the man needed help, he was just turning his back on him.

Maybe it was time to return the favor.

Of course, he had no way of being absolutely sure that he had been offered and then hired for this job because of anything the professor might have done or said. Still, it *was* a feeling he had because of a few things that Harrison had said to him in passing. He had to admit that this particular job paid a lot better than the one he'd just left.

Not to mention that working here carried with it another little bonus. Being on the campus had awakened something inside him that had been dormant for a very long time. The desire to take charge of his life, to get back to the halls of learning and make something more of himself than someone who just shuffled aimlessly through life.

That, too, he thought, had been because of something the professor had said to him. Not just the remark about his future, but other things. Meaningful things that carried with them no recriminations, but made him stop and think nonetheless. He hadn't acted on his feelings because he had come to accept his way of life and doing something about it would mean another upheaval. But that wasn't Harrison's fault.

She was right. The professor was too good a guy to abandon in his time of need. But that still didn't cancel out his moral dilemma.

The phrase "caught between a rock and a hard place" took on new meaning for him.

With a sigh, Smith turned around to look at Jane. And found that she was a lot closer than he'd anticipated. Instead of being in her doorway, she was right there. His body brushed up against hers when he turned.

What felt curiously like a zigzag of electricity coursed through his veins. Just like that time he'd accidentally touched a live wire.

Smith took a step back, trying not to look like a man who had just been on the receiving end of one hell of a jolt.

"Smith? Did the professor ever help you?"

Reining himself in, Smith put her plant down for the second time and fixed her with a look. "How did you know about that?"

So, she'd been right, Jane thought in satisfaction as she tried to catch her breath. Right and also electrocuted. What *was* that, anyway? She hadn't expected him to turn around when he did, certain he'd just keep on walking. She'd meant to stop him in his tracks. Instead he'd all but knocked her off hers.

She cleared her throat, hoping she didn't sound like some squeaky-voiced ninny.

"Just a guess." If she was going to get the man to side with her, she knew she was going to have to be strictly honest with him. That meant she couldn't pretend to know something about him she didn't. "The professor has helped a lot of us in one way or another." Saying it out loud gave her another idea. "I think maybe Broadstreet knows and is jealous of that."

"Of the professor's helping students?" That would be the last thing he'd guess.

Jane shook her head. She wasn't being very articulate, she upbraided herself. "No, of the good will that everyone bears Professor Harrison."

Smith snorted. "If everyone bore Harrison all this so-called 'good will,' they wouldn't be trying to get rid of him now, would they?"

She'd already thought that out. "That's Broadstreet's work," she reminded him. "The others on the board are probably afraid to cross him. It might mean their jobs if they do, or at the very least, their position on the board." She thought of the various members. Not a hero in the lot. Her eyes settled on Smith as the word "hero" echoed in her head. "They've all got a lot to lose."

His eyes narrowed. There it was again, that prejudice he'd been fighting against, in one form or another, all of his life. He would have thought that she wouldn't be guilty of it, but then, he'd been wrong before. A lot. "And I don't?"

Where had he come up with that? Was he really that thin-skinned or was she missing something? "I didn't mean to imply that."

And now she was going to backpedal and come up with excuses, Smith thought. Well, he didn't want to hear them. He knew better.

"Sure you did. You figure I'm just some lowly maintenance guy. I lose this job, I'll find another one, mucking out some other bathrooms, in no time."

She felt her temper flaring. Damn it, Smith really made her angry. Angry over the waste of a life she saw, angry over his attitude. And angry because she felt almost powerless to help the professor, one of the few decent people she'd ever encounter. She didn't even know if there was anything in the files that might be useful, but she couldn't get to them if Smith didn't help her.

He began to turn away from her and she grabbed his arm, forcing him to look at her. He looked surprised by her action and she felt a smattering of triumph over that. "You know, if you take that damn twelve-foot chip off your shoulder, you might be able to move faster."

He loomed over her then, his brow furrowing like thunder about to crash over the terrain. Certainly over her. She stuck her chin out, as if daring him to contradict her.

"What did you just say?"

For once Jane didn't falter, didn't back away from her position. She'd done enough of that all her life, especially with Drew. Being on her own now, having to take care of not just herself but her son, as well, with no magnanimous, mysterious benefactor waiting in the wings to come to her rescue the way he or she had back when she was in college, had forced her to strengthen her backbone. Or at least to find it. She realized that it had been among the missing for far too long.

"I said you should get rid of the chip on your shoulder, Smith. The universe doesn't just revolve around you."

He'd never thought that it had. But ever since he'd been falsely accused and swiftly convicted at the court of public opinion, he'd felt like the universe's whipping boy. Something he figured Jane had never had to deal with. She looked as if the hardest decisions she encountered was which shade of nail polish to buy. "What the hell would you know about it?"

She resented his tone. Did he think he had a lock on problems? At least *he* hadn't wasted precious years locked into a terrible marriage and watched the person he loved betray him time and again. Or worse, abuse him.

Anger mixed with pride in her eyes. "I know that everyone has setbacks. I certainly did. But you move on. You take charge, take command of your life and *do* something about it."

Empty words. Easy to say when they had nothing to do with you, he thought. He had no idea why he didn't just ignore her and walk away. "And what do you propose I do about my life?"

It was a challenge. She didn't know if he was actually asking, or telling her to back off. The old Jane would have backed off in a New York minute, fabricating excuses as she tripped over her own tongue. She would have told herself she was just being polite, just trying not to hurt anyone's feelings, but the real reason would have been that she hadn't the courage to say something that might actually put her in conflict with another human being.

But that was the old Jane. The new Jane had battles to fight.

Starting here, starting now.

"What do I propose you do about your life?" she repeated. He was still glaring at her. Her pulse began to race, but she wouldn't back down. She couldn't. "Stop feeling sorry for yourself, for one. Find a way to go back and get your education."

It took effort not to sneer at her. "Oh, just like that?"

He was ridiculing her. Her back went up. She wasn't about to take that from him.

"No, not just like that," she shot back. "But lots of people a lot older than you go back to school to get their diploma. They go at night, or on weekends, or whenever they can, but they *go*. They *do* something," she insisted. "You're too smart just to work a plunger for the rest of your life, Smith." He was about to tell her where she could put that plunger, she could see it in his eyes. Jane talked faster. "If you were happy doing it, then that's fine. But you're not happy."

Smith set his jaw hard. For a little thing, Jane had a hell of a lot of nerve. He didn't know why he didn't resent it more than he did.

"And how would you know that?"

He was kidding, right? Had the man looked into a mirror recently? "If you were happy, you wouldn't walk around looking as if you'd just consumed a mouthful of rotten eggs."

Now there was one he hadn't heard before. "You've gotten more colorful since I sat next to you. And a lot pushier."

She'd been prepared for something a great deal more caustic than that. Jane released the breath she was holding. "Yes, I have. And you didn't sit next to me," she corrected. "You sat two rows over." His desk had been parallel to hers. His right profile had been the first thing she'd noticed. It looked as if it had been chiseled out of rock.

Smith raised an eyebrow, surprised. "You remember that?"

The air felt warm between them as she looked up at him. "I remember that." And then, because she didn't want him getting the wrong idea—or the right one—she quickly added, "I remember a lot of things. One of which was that you were one of the smartest guys I ever ran into. And then suddenly you weren't."

He didn't need to be reminded of that. Smith shrugged dismissively. "It happens."

There was no arguing with that. But she didn't think he had the right outlook on it. "It happens for a reason. When my parents were killed, my grades almost tanked completely. Not to mention that there was no money for me to continue my education—"

He looked at her sharply. "Then how—?"

"I'll tell you how," she interrupted. "The professor took an interest in me. He made it a point to raise my spirits." And she would be forever grateful to him for that. "To make me see that my parents would have wanted me to continue and, out of respect for them, I had to be the best I could be. So I was."

Life had taught him to be practical. "What about the money?"

"That came from an account that was mysteriously set up for me. It paid my tuition and my room and board at the university. I took a job so I could have some spending money. But I always felt that the professor might have somehow had something to do with that mysterious account."

Smith stared at her. "You think he secretly opened up the account?" It would seem to him more straightforward just to either give or loan her the money, not be almost underhanded about it. What purpose did that serve?

She shook her head. "No, I think it was more along the lines of his having some kind of access to a foundation, or maybe he knew some publicity-shy benefactor who had too much money on his hands and was looking to do a good deed. I don't really know," she admitted, "but I'd bet anything I have that the professor was behind that account in some way." A sadness filled her. "Which makes what's going on that much more terrible. His wife just died eight months ago. He's lost without her. If they make him leave the university, it may just kill him."

"The man's made of tougher stuff than that."

She looked at Smith pointedly. "We all have a breaking point. This might be his. If he stops being who he's been for these last thirty years, I'm afraid the professor's going to wither away and die."

Smith looked at her skeptically. "That's being kind of melodramatic, isn't it?"

She didn't think so. "Melodrama has its place, too, and in this case, I think that it's true." Smith was listening to her, she thought. She had him. Now all she had to do was reel him in. "All that man has is us, this place, these students." She gestured around the hallway. "He's sent for some of his former students to come and speak on his behalf to the board when they're finally ready to convene."

Then she didn't need the old files or him. "Well, that should be enough."

But Jane wasn't convinced. "I'd rather we had a lot of backup information to fall back on than to be caught short. Sandra Westport came to me today—"

"That cheerleader who married the jock?" Both had been considered part of the in-crowd when he was at Saunders. He had no use for either.

The cheerleader and the jock. It sounded like the title of a 1940's movie. Jane couldn't help the smile that came to her lips. "One and the same. Sandra writes for some neighborhood newspaper now. Getting into the files was her idea."

His eyes never left hers. "And was asking me for the keys also her idea?"

"No, that was mine," she freely admitted. Sandra had just assumed that she could easily get to the files without any trouble. But then, Sandra's life was probably one of those trouble-free existences where everything went right just because she was Sandra Westport. "I don't think she even knows you work here."

He scowled. "I won't be if anyone finds out I gave you the keys."

Jane paused, regrouping. She certainly didn't want him getting into trouble over this. The point was saving jobs, not losing them.

"Look, you don't have to hand the keys to me. Just leave them lying around somewhere where I can get to them." She glanced at the key ring that hung off his belt.

She hadn't realized how many keys there were. "Or just the one for the basement. That way—"

He filled in the rest for her. "I can say that I didn't have anything to do with breaking into the room in the basement, besides being careless with my keys?"

It sounded lame when he said it. But right now she had nothing else. Jane shrugged. "Something like that."

"The coward's way out." His expression was unfathomable.

"Not cowardly," she protested quickly, sensing that he'd balk at the term. "Safe." And then, because she couldn't help herself, she added, "The way you've been playing things since you left the university."

He regarded her in silence for a long moment. "Nice dig."

She'd crossed over the line, Jane thought. She didn't want him angry, just motivated. "Sorry. I get a little out of line when I get passionate."

"That's a lot out of line," he corrected, his eyes steely, "and I didn't notice you getting passionate," Smith told her. "What I noticed was that you were getting fairly worked up."

She didn't see his point. "Same thing."

Hooking his thumbs in his belt, Smith shook his head. "Not in my book."

Passionate had a completely different meaning for him. Passionate involved the heart in matters that were strictly male-female, not causes, such as saving venerable professors' jobs. Passionate might have once been used to describe the way he'd felt about her

Her phone was ringing, reminding her that she had

a desk full of work to attended to and that she wasn't being paid to stand in the hallway and argue with an obstinate male.

But for the moment she stood her ground. This had to be resolved before she could turn her attention to anything else. Otherwise, she wouldn't be able to focus.

"So, will you do it? Will you leave your keys lying around?"

"No."

She closed her eyes, searching for strength. "Smith—" When she opened them again, she saw that he was looking directly at her.

"But I will unlock the door," he told her evenly. Then surprised the hell out of her by adding, "And stay with you."

If someone stumbled across her, she could come up with something plausible. She didn't think whatever she created could stretch to cover both of them. "That's not necessary."

This was nonnegotiable. "It is in my book. I can't leave you alone down there." He sounded immovable as he added, "Wouldn't be right."

She regarded him for a long moment, clearly not knowing what to make of him or how to read him. "I guess chivalry's not dead."

He shrugged carelessly. "Don't know about chivalry, but I wouldn't want you on my conscience."

She tried to make sense of his comment and could only draw one conclusion. "You think something could happen to me down there?"

For the first time she saw his mouth curve into what

could only be termed as a grin. "You've never seen any of those horror movies? The ones where the beautiful woman creeps around in a dusty campus sub-basement and is found the next morning with her soul missing?"

She'd never been into horror movies as a teenager. She'd never seen the point in willingly allowing herself to be frightened. "These days I only get to watch movies where all the characters are animated and the animals talk, walk upright and wear clothes."

Beautiful, she thought, the word suddenly coming back to her. Had he just called her beautiful? Or was Smith just referring to the heroines in those movies in general?

Didn't matter, she told herself. What mattered was that he'd just agreed to help her.

Sounded as if she doted on her son, Smith thought. His mother had been like that. Actually, both his parents had. Looking back, he knew he'd been one of the lucky ones when he was growing up. His had been a happy home life.

"You need to get out more," he commented.

"I will be. To the archives. Thanks to you," she added with a smile. "I can't do it tonight. I promised Danny I'd take him to one of those kid restaurants for dinner. How about tomorrow night, are you free then?" She realized that she was taking a lot for granted. "Or, if you're busy, I could—"

His days and nights had a sameness to them that left them indistinguishable from one another, blending into the weekends without leaving any sign of their passage anywhere. This wasn't earth-shattering, but a little covert detective work would shake things up somewhat, he imagined.

"No," he told her, cutting Jane short, "I'm not busy."

Her eyes lit up, looking almost translucent. "Great." She thought for a second. "I'll stay behind after the professor leaves. If he asks me why, I'll just tell him I'm still catching up on some of the work that piled up while I was gone on vacation. You can come by and meet me here after six. He's usually gone by then."

He shook his head. The woman sounded as if she was planning a bank heist. "Got it all worked out, don't you?"

She still didn't know how to take him. Was he being sarcastic? Or was this just the way Smith Parker had turned out? "It's not exactly an elaborate plan."

No, but there was something to be said for simplicity. The simpler something was, the less likely slipups would occur.

Jane had aroused his curiosity. "And what would you have done if I'd said no?"

That was easy. "Worked on you until you said yes," she told him honestly.

He supposed by agreeing he'd just saved himself a great deal of irritation. "You think I'm that easily worn down?"

The opposite was true. "Nobody said anything about easy. As a matter of fact, I didn't think you'd agree as fast as you did."

He liked the way her whole body became animated when she spoke, as if every piece, every joint, was in concert with her thoughts. He couldn't remember when he'd witnessed that kind of enthusiasm.

"I could say no again," he deadpanned.

He was kidding, right? Looking at his expression, she wasn't sure. "Don't you dare."

And then he laughed and she felt relief washing over her. A moment before she felt something stir inside. The man not only had an incredibly sexy voice, but his laugh was positively sinful. Like some deep, dark melody that pulled at something very basic, very primal, within her.

"Don't worry, I won't," he promised. His expression softened ever so slightly. She remembered how handsome he'd seemed to her. "You're right. The professor's a good guy. He doesn't deserve to be put through all this just because he's not streamlined and high-tech oriented. Some things high tech can't replace."

She firmly believed that herself, but was surprised to hear him voice her opinion. "Such as?"

He never hesitated. "Compassion."

And here she thought he was so full of anger, so self-oriented he couldn't see anything else. "You're the last person I would have thought would say that."

"Yeah, well, I'm just chock-full of surprises." And so was she, he thought. He would have never thought of her as being spirited. Because looking into her eyes was suddenly too disturbing, he glanced down at her plant. "Now, if you're through recruiting me into a life of crime, I have a tree to save."

She moved out of the way as he picked the fig tree up in one arm and hefted the toolbox with the other. "Will you bring it back once you're done?"

"Maybe," was all he said as he walked away.

Definitely an odd man, Jane thought.

But before she could contemplate him further, the phone began to ring again, and she was off and running back to her day.

Chapter Six

The shadow unexpectedly falling across her desk made Jane jump.

"So much for nerves of steel," Smith commented, walking into her office.

Jane flushed slightly, annoyed with herself for being so jumpy, annoyed with Smith for noticing. "I was preoccupied."

It was six-fifteen. The professor had gone home for the night a little more than ten minutes ago. Before leaving, he'd asked her what she was doing, staying on after hours. The flimsy excuse she'd given him about not feeling right until she'd finished inputting some data had felt incredibly transparent to her, but the professor seemed to accept it, cautioning her not to stay too late.

She hated lying. But she had a feeling that Professor

Harrison wouldn't stand for her breaking or even bending any rules on his account.

Which made her that much more determined to bend them. People like the professor didn't just grow on trees.

Smith watched as the woman's fingers flew over the keyboard, closing whatever it was she'd been working on and shutting down the computer for the night. It made a farewell noise as the monitor faded to black.

"You ready?" Smith doled out the words slowly, as if he was dealing cards at a table filled with hesitant betters.

Finished, now that her heart was back to beating normally, Jane looked at him again. Instead of the navy coveralls she'd come to expect on him, he was wearing a pair of light-colored jeans and a short-sleeved navy pullover sweater. Though not tight, the sweater allowed all the muscles that were beneath to be displayed.

The man worked out, she thought. He'd filled out some since they'd been students here. And she'd forgotten how good he looked in civilian clothes.

"Ready," she announced, rising from the desk. In less than a minute, she was on the other side of her office door, locking it. She pushed the strap of her purse back up onto her shoulder. "Let's go."

They entered the administration building through the back entrance, where supply deliveries were periodically made. From there, it was a short distance to the stairwell. They took it down to the basement to avoid running into anyone.

Her heels echoing on the concrete floor, she felt incredibly nefarious as she followed Smith to the locked door.

"You might have thought of wearing rubber soles instead of shoes that tap out Morse code," he upbraided her.

"I'm new at being sneaky." Jane whispered the words as she watched him unlock the door.

Turning the knob, he walked in ahead of her.

Slightly used daylight pushed its way in through windows that had last been washed approximately a decade ago. The room was dank and smelled of settled dust. It was crammed with rows of metal file cabinets that contained the academic lives and who knew what else of students who had long since left these halls.

The task felt daunting.

She gave herself to the count of five to rally. She made it by three. Jane looked around for a light switch.

"Over there." Smith pointed, anticipating her.

Crossing to the wall, she flipped the switch on. Illumination added to the depression rather than subtracted from it. She was aware of Smith watching her every move. It made her self-conscious.

"Looks like they're arranged by year of graduation," he said, glancing down the first row.

She nodded. "Yes, I know."

Bracing herself for what was going to be a very long night, she approached a row of files to orient herself as to their year. Smith shadowed her.

She opened a file cabinet, then looked at him. "You

really don't have to be here, you know. I promise not to steal anything."

They obviously had opposing views about the necessity of his presence. "Look, it's my butt on the line if anyone finds out that you're down here, searching through the files."

The cabinet was labeled 1962. Too early. She moved to another row. "Don't worry, if anyone finds out, I wouldn't tell them I got the keys from you."

It wasn't that simple. "My building, my responsibility."

"This isn't some office in the basement of the CIA headquarters," she pointed out, humor curving her lips in what Smith viewed to be an enticing manner. "There are probably several other people with keys to this place." Nineteen sixty-seven, she read. Still too early. Jane moved on to the next row. "No one's about to torture me to find out who my source is—and why should anyone find me here in the first place? I'm looking through files, not having a rave. The odds are excellent that no one will ever be aware that I was even down here—until I find what I'm looking for." *Whatever that is,* she added silently.

But Smith looked far from convinced. "The unexpected happens."

There was something in his voice that caught her attention. She didn't know why, but she knew his reference wasn't just some vague comment about the whimsy of fate, it was about his scholarship being suddenly yanked out from under him.

She stopped working her way down the aisles and looked at him for a moment. She'd never gotten any real details about what had actually happened, although everyone had a different idea at the time. The consensus was that Smith had been caught stealing things from several of the girls' dorm rooms.

Her eyes met his. "You mean, like losing your scholarship?"

He couldn't tell from her tone whether she was being sarcastic, accusatory or something else. "Yeah, like that."

Was he guilty? Granted he'd been young at the time, but he hadn't been stupid, no matter how much he might have needed the money. What could have possessed Smith to do it?

"You had to know that you were taking a risk." He looked at her sharply and her courage flagged. But then, she told herself that she'd begun this, she might as well see it through to its conclusion. If she was wrong, it was about time he set her and everyone else, especially Administration, straight.

Now that it was in the past, he'd promised himself that he would never dignify the accusations by denying them or defending himself. And yet, when she'd said it, he felt compelled to stand up for himself.

"I wasn't taking any kind of a risk. Except maybe in believing that things were going to turn out all right."

His voice was almost ominously low. Alarms went off in her head, telling her to back away. To leave the subject alone. That she was only asking for trouble by bringing it up.

But she wasn't asking for trouble, she was asking for

an explanation. For a clue as to the inner workings of the man who was inadvertently blocking her access to the next row of files.

With a wave of her hand, she moved him to the side and went down to the next row. Looking for a starting point. The glue on the label affixed to the next drawer had long since dried up. The label was missing. She opened the drawer and looked inside.

Nineteen seventy-nine. Getting warmer. She wanted to go through as many student files as she could, starting from the beginning of the professor's career at the university.

She raised an eyebrow as she cocked it in Smith's direction. "Then you didn't take anything from the girls' dorms?"

His lips became a compressed, tight line.

She had no way of knowing that he was holding back a torment of hot, angry words, words he'd never been able to release over the injustice of having been convicted before he was ever even formally charged. Convicted in the public's eyes without being able to make a case for himself.

But anger over that burst to the surface now. "What the hell would I want from the girls' dormitories?"

She gave him the logical litany. "Money, jewelry, books you could resell."

He didn't think along those lines. Obviously she did. He looked at her now, wondering if *she* had ever stolen anything. "You sound like you've made more of a study of it than I ever did."

She thought back to her days on the campus. "Things went missing."

His eyes narrowed. Was it her imagination, or was he standing closer to her than he had been just a minute ago? Should she be worried? Jane searched his eyes, looking for signs she'd come to know all too well, signs she'd seen in Drew's eyes. Just before he'd hit her.

"Things might have gone missing, but I never touched them," he said evenly.

The anger she saw appeared suppressed. Maybe the stale air in the basement was making her light-headed, but she heard herself pressing on. "You were seen coming out of the building around the same time that the thefts were said to have occurred."

Said to have occurred. He didn't doubt that the events had been orchestrated. That he had been framed. Not that anyone would ever believe him. He called himself a fool even as he framed his answer.

"A lot of guys were seen coming and going from the girls' floor. The buildings weren't exactly locked down tight the way they were in the fifties," he pointed out. He knew he was talking down to her and he didn't care. People had been talking down to him for half his life. But he nonetheless stopped himself and looked at her. "Are you deliberately trying to get on my bad side?"

She couldn't help the half-smile. Maybe it was even a nervous reaction that coupled itself with the comment that came to her lips.

"Until a little bit ago," she told him candidly, "I didn't know there was a good side."

He supposed that he did come across as surly, but there was a reason for that. One he wasn't about to apologize for. If she didn't like it, it was too damn bad. "Look—"

But she was already holding up her hand. The last thing she wanted to do was to waste time arguing with him. Or to give offense. After all, if it wasn't for him, she wouldn't be down here.

"Sorry." She grabbed at any excuse, wanting to smooth things out. "I'm just trying to find out some things about you."

Suspicion replaced the early, fine lines around his mouth and eyes that the sun had awarded him for all the hours he stayed outdoors, working in both his garden and his parents'.

"Why?"

He looked incredibly intense, incredibly leery. Okay, the best way out of this was humor, Jane decided. "Because, like it or not, we're now involved. You have my fig tree, I have your key. If we were still in college, we'd be close to being a couple." His expression did not change. When he continued to stare at her as if she'd lost her mind, she cleared her throat. "Just trying to lighten the air a little."

He snorted. The air felt like a lighter version of lead. He wondered what breathing this in on a regular basis could do to a person's lungs. If she was planning to do this more than just this once, he was going to have to see about getting a fan down here and pointing it toward the window to suck out the stale air and dust before she came down with something.

"Forget about the air," he instructed sternly. "Just get to what you're supposed to be doing."

1975. Bingo! The year Professor Harrison arrived at Saunders. She opened the drawer, knowing the task ahead of her was still going to be monumental.

She looked at Smith. "This isn't going to take a few minutes," she warned him. "At a minimum, this is going to take a week. Probably several," she added, cautiously watching his reaction.

Smith scowled. He didn't like the sound of that. "I didn't sign on for that."

"I know." She didn't want to put him out and she really didn't like the feeling of having Smith hovering over her. "Maybe if you could make me my own copy of the key—"

Was she out of her mind? "Why don't I also have the school cafeteria send over dinner trays for you while I'm at it?"

Okay, she'd been polite enough. "There's no reason for sarcasm."

Yes, there was. She was prying into his life and sarcasm was just about his only weapon, he thought. "There's no reason for this, either." He waved a hand around the area. Metal file cabinets stood like rusting sentries "You don't even know what you're looking for, do you?"

"Something to use in the professor's defense." Since she'd approached Smith for his help, she'd gone back through some of the professor's class lists, compiling the names of his students to help narrow down her scope. She was still toying with several ideas. "Maybe a comparison of how his students did academically as opposed to the rest of the students."

That definitely didn't apply to him, although it certainly had nothing to do with lack of the professor's influence. "Well then, you'd better not include me," he told her.

Taking out a file, she skimmed it, then set it aside on top of the file cabinet. One down, a hundred to go, she mused. She glanced in Smith's direction. "You're the exception that proves the rule."

He'd never understood that expression. "What the hell does that mean?"

Rather than resort to some kind of convoluted logic, she flashed a grin at him.

"Haven't a clue." Before he could ask, she added, "I tend to babble when I'm nervous."

He glanced over his shoulder toward the door. Jane made her way down to the next drawer. "Breaking and entering tends to make me nervous, too."

Squatting, she looked up at him before resuming her search. "That's not why I'm nervous." She replayed his words in her head and drew her own conclusion. "So you *have* done this kind of thing before."

"No, and if you're trying to trip me up, Colombo, you failed." It had been meant strictly as a quip. Obviously she'd put her own inference on it. "I was seen coming out of the girls' section at the dorm because I had gone there to drop off a note."

If that was the case, it would have been easy enough to prove. Why hadn't he? "No one ever came forward to say you were there visiting them."

He looked at her for a long moment, wondering what she'd say if she knew that he had gone there that day to see her. Both of them had been shy as hell and he'd finally worked up his courage to make the first move, only to find that she wasn't there.

Feeling as if maybe that was an omen, he'd retreated and gone back to work.

"That's because the person I went to see wasn't there." And he wasn't about to explain it any further than that. "Look, that happened a long time ago and it's not something I like thinking about—"

She'd learned from experience that sweeping things under the rug only got you a lumpy rug. You had to confront the things that were wrong in your life, no matter how hard it was.

"Maybe you should," she suggested. By the expression on his face, she knew she wasn't making points. Jane pressed on anyway. "Once and for all. Try to clear your name with the board." She went back to reading names across the tops of the files. "Then go on with the rest of your life."

She was pandering to him, he thought, and he hated being patronized. "Oh, so now you think I'm not guilty."

The look in her eyes, he thought, was pure innocence. It threw him. "You just said you weren't."

Still, he wasn't about to let himself be lulled into taking things at face value. She had to have some kind of ulterior motive.

"And you believe me."

"Yes, why shouldn't I?" She stopped flipping through files and looked at him, her pale green eyes pinning him down far better than any nail gun. "You're not lying, right?"

His face hardened. She was good, he thought. He almost believed that she was being sincere. "You have no way of knowing that."

Taking out a second file, she closed the drawer. When she had enough files, she intended to scan the pages that were pertinent and then return them to their drawers before going on. Right now, she looked at Smith. "Why are you trying to make me change my mind? Don't you like having people in your corner?"

Was that what it was? Was she in his corner? Or did she just want him to think so? God, looking at that innocent face, he could almost...

He frowned. "Just not used to it, that's all."

She had a theory about that. "Maybe that's because you push everyone away."

Impatient, uncomfortable, Smith shoved his hands into his pockets and glared at her. "Look, I thought you wanted to find something to help the professor—"

She knew what he was going to say. She was convinced that men were just not as good at multitasking as women were. Women had invented it. It had originally been called motherhood.

"I can talk and look at the same time."

Yeah, he supposed she could. But he didn't want her continuing on this path. It was his business, not hers. "Go a lot faster if you concentrated."

She had never reacted well to criticism. Drew had criticized her all the time and it had left some very raw spots on her psyche.

"I *am* concentrating."

Smith blew out a breath and glanced toward one of the windows that ran along the top of one wall. Since the school year hadn't officially begun, the normal foot traffic, even at this hour, was absent. He saw nothing but the vague outline of grass that was due to go into hibernation soon.

Restless, he leaned against one of the file cabinets. A spider scurried along his arm, seeking somewhere less public to spin its web.

"So what does make you nervous?"

The question seemed to come out of the blue. She paused in her search through a bottom drawer. "What?"

"You said breaking and entering wasn't what was making you nervous. That makes it sound that there's something else. What?"

Getting up, Jane pushed the file drawer closed with her foot. This was going to be *really* slow going. "You," she said honestly. She saw that she'd taken him by surprise. "You're so angry, you look as if you're going to explode."

There were times when he thought he might. But then he reined himself in, telling himself none of it made any difference. At times, he actually succeeded in convincing himself.

"Wouldn't you be angry if you were me?"

There was no question about that. "Sure. But I would have used that anger as a tool to help me prove my innocence."

Easy for her to say. She hadn't lived through it. "Nobody was willing to listen."

She knew better. He'd had a built in advocate and he probably hadn't even used him. "The professor would have. Did you go to him when this happened?"

That would have been begging. He didn't have much, but he had his pride. *What's your pride doing for you these days?* a small voice asked. He had no answer for that. Only more anger.

"I don't need to have people fight my battles for me."

She didn't see it that way. Resuming her search, she worked her way down to the next row. Smith drifted after her.

"You do if you don't fight them yourself." Finding another folder she could use, she pulled it out, then looked at him. "You just gave up, didn't you? Dropped out because you were insulted that someone—that *anyone*—could think that way about you."

She'd hit it right on the head. It only made him angrier. "I don't like being psychoanalyzed."

Didn't he get it? She was on his side. "You should like being falsely accused even less."

He didn't want to stand around to listen to any more of this. But he couldn't very well just walk off and leave her down here, either. For two reasons. Because he believed that no place was really safe for a female alone at night. And because, since she was using his keys, she was his responsibility. Not that he expected her to steal anything the way she'd laughingly suggested. But to leave the keys out of his line of vision was careless and he'd never been that.

There was only one thing left to do.

"Look, maybe this'll go faster if there's two of us." He vaguely knew what she was looking for. "I'll look through those files over there." He pointed to a row on the other side of the small, dusty room.

She more than welcomed the help. And maybe she'd be better off if he wasn't standing so close to her like this. That old attraction she'd once felt toward him seemed to be enjoying its own revival. It made concentrating on what she was doing rather difficult.

"Okay, just make sure you don't go back more than about thirty years," she cautioned as he began to walk off. "That's when the professor started working here."

"That's the year before I was born," he commented. The professor had been here his entire lifetime. His own work history already included more places than the professor had on his résumé. Smith couldn't conceive being anywhere that long. Maybe because he hadn't found somewhere he wanted to be that long, he thought.

"Me, too," she replied, back at work. "Hard concept to really wrap your mind around, isn't it?" He looked at her. Feeling his eyes on her, Jane looked up, pausing again. "Professor Harrison was married to his wife even longer than that." She sighed, unaware that it sounded wistful. "Imagine loving someone for that long and then being without them. And now Broadstreet is trying to separate him from his life's work, too."

Maybe she was putting too dramatic a spin on this. "People retire."

Yes, but they weren't talking about people, they were talking about the professor. Who clearly didn't want to retire.

"The ones who retire willingly retire *to* something, or hate what they're doing so much that even doing nothing is preferable to it. That's not the professor in either case. He loves what he does. It's who he is. 'The Professor.' If they force him to retire, force him out of his office, then he stops being 'The Professor,' at least in his own mind, and I'm afraid that's a very dangerous place for him to be right now."

She sighed. The man tried to keep up a good front,

but she knew him too well. She could see into him, into his heart. "He still hasn't recovered over losing his wife," she repeated. "Besides, if he has to leave Saunders, he has to give up his house, as well. So in one blink of an eye, he'd find himself widowed, jobless and homeless." Any one of those was too terrible to contemplate. As a one-two-three punch, it was permanently crippling.

Jane looked at Smith, wondering if she was getting through to him. His expression gave her no indication. "*Now* do you see why I'm trying so hard to help him?"

She still hadn't said the professor had said as much to her. That meant she was reading into the situation. "Because you like to meddle would have been my guess."

"Help," she corrected firmly. "Not meddle, *help.*"

Smith gave a careless shrug as he pulled out a bunch of files and glanced at the front of each to where the classes and grades were recorded for each semester. Rather than a neat computer printout the way there was these days, the transcript was handwritten, and rather poorly at that.

He looked through the first file, then returned it. "So, who's watching your kid?"

The personal question took her by surprise. Maybe she was making headway, she thought.

"I have a next-door neighbor who dotes on him. She's a grandmother whose own grandchildren live in another state. So she pours out all those grandmotherly feelings she has onto Danny." Sometimes nature balances things out. "Which is great because he doesn't have a grandmother of his own."

He returned two more files to their place. "Your husband doesn't have parents?"

"Ex-husband," she corrected with emphasis. "And looking back, I think he was probably raised by wolves. That would account for his wandering behavior at any rate."

He read between the lines. "Wrong species."

She pushed the drawer closed, then opened the next one, trying not to think how many more drawers she was going to have to go through. "What?"

Her ex probably cheated on her. Though why, he couldn't understand. If he and Jane had gotten together when he'd first fallen for her, there would be no way he would have ever walked away from her. He would have loved her to his last breath...

Smith let it drop. No sense in going there. "Wolves are monogamous," he told her. "You're probably thinking of rabbits or bears. They'll mate with anything that crosses their path."

That would be Drew, she thought. Then banished him from her mind. She couldn't waste time thinking about a man who wasn't worth the trouble. Instead she looked toward Smith.

"How would you—?"

He second-guessed her question. "The Discovery Channel," he told her. "The station of choice for the discerning insomniac."

Pushing the drawer closed, she didn't open a new one. "You have insomnia?"

"Sometimes."

When he thought about where his life wasn't going and where it might have gone if someone like Jacob Weber hadn't messed it up. He knew why Jacob had done it. Because he'd been privy to the secret Jacob had tried so hard to hide. And, for the most part, Jacob had been successful in keeping his secret.

But he had seen the premed student coming out of a thrift shop, counting money. Rich kids didn't go to thrift shops, except on a lark and then to buy, not sell. You only sold things to a thrift shop if you needed money.

Which meant that Jacob hadn't been the rich kid everyone'd believed him to be.

Their eyes had met that day. There'd been fear and then hatred in Jacob's. Shortly thereafter, the accusation against him had materialized. To keep his secret, to keep his own life intact, Jacob had seen fit to ruin Smith's.

Sure, he could have fought it, the way Jane said, but it would have been his word against Jacob's if anyone would have allowed it to come down to that. And Jacob Weber was thought to be a golden boy, while he'd been just the son of blue collar people, there on a work-study scholarship.

The verdict was in before a single accusation was leveled.

"But to answer your question, no." Jane went on as she walked down to another row. "As far as I know, my ex-husband's father's dead and his mother lives in Canada." Not that the woman even deserved the term. "She didn't even bother coming to our wedding, or to send so much as a card when he sent her the announcement that Danny was born." Her mouth curved in an ironic smile. "Not exactly the warm-and-toasty type. Certainly not the kind of grandmother who bakes cookies and reads bedtime stories. Gladys is."

"Gladys?"

"My neighbor. I think if I let her, she'd be happy to adopt Danny."

She had a built-in baby-sitter, Smith thought. "That must free you up, so you can kick up your heels if you want."

She couldn't tell if that was an accusation or just idle conversation. "I'm very happy with my heels right where they are—on the ground," she informed him curtly.

Jane was around the corner. He could hear her closing one drawer and opening another. Had he insulted her? For a second he thought of going around the aisle and apologizing, then decided against it. He wasn't here to socialize. He was here to make sure the professor got more of a break than he had.

Blocking out thoughts of the woman in the next row, Smith got back to work.

Chapter Seven

Alexander Broadstreet frowned to himself as he filled the chunky glass on his custom-made bar with aged-old Scotch.

The best for the best, he thought.

It wasn't his first drink of the evening, but then, it had been a particularly trying day. He needed something to cut the edge off the anger that was smoldering within him before it erupted.

Things were not going according to plan.

He took a long sip of the bitter amber liquid. It didn't help his mood any more than the first two drinks had.

Damn it, he'd been certain that after Harrison's wife's death that hopeless throwback would have been easily gotten rid of. Didn't a lovebird die after its lifelong mate expired? Harrison and his wife had been sicken-

ingly devoted to one another. Harrison had always said
at those awful faculty parties that without her he was
only half a person.

Certainly he had expected no opposition from the
man when he had tactfully suggested that perhaps Harrison had outlived his usefulness to the university and
should make way for someone more attuned to the
board's policies.

God knew that the man both looked and behaved as
if he were straight out of the eighties. Completely passé.
Broadstreet took another long sip, waiting for the mel-
lowness to hit. Harrison definitely did *not* embody the
kind of image he and the board were trying to project
for Saunders.

Athletics was bigger business now than ever and
money was what kept a university going. Saunders University *needed* to attract the jocks, the future sports
moneymakers of the next decade, not scholars who
brought nothing to the table but their books. Star athletes brought money. They could always be counted on
to open their bulging pockets to fund another wing, another scholarship. And put Saunders back in the news.
On the first few pages of the local newspaper.

And he, as the head of the board, was always right
there in the photograph. In the public's eye. Where he
both wanted and needed to be. He took another long sip,
his lips twitching in a humorless smile as memories
crowded his mind. Ironic that the geek who couldn't
make any team should be kept in the public's eye because the school he headed could produce so many
champion athletes.

Outstanding baseball players, football stars, giants of the basketball court, Saunders University had more than its share. And would continue to do so if he had anything to say about it. Recruitment was intense. He had his scouts out all over the country, watching promising high school seniors, approaching the cream of the crop with veiled promises of an easy four years and a prestigious diploma. Most of the teachers he spoke to at Saunders were on board with his plans.

The one anchor holding them back was Harrison. Harrison, who insisted on repeatedly playing the same damn note over and over again: that the university's emphasis was in the wrong place.

Wrong place, he snorted. The damn fool had been a coach, he should know better. But even as a coach, Harrison had emphasized that learning came before playing. He'd even kept a few key players away from crucial games over the years because they'd failed one or another exam.

Learning before playing, Broadstreet sneered, his hand tightening on the glass. As if that could bring the money in.

The door to his den opened without the benefit of a knock first. His wife, Alicia stood in the doorway, her elegant personal-trainer-toned body resplendent in a basic black dress that showcased every hard won curve.

The only curve to her mouth was a deep frown as she looked at the glass he held in his hand.

"I'm driving."

A mirthless smile automatically took possession of Broadstreet's lips. It was the same smile he wore when glad-handing potential donors at a university fund-raiser. Except that there as a flinty edge to it. "I never thought otherwise, dear."

Alicia blew out an angry breath. "It's amazing you can think at all, given the fact that you spend so much time pickling your brain."

His eyes darkened even though his expression never changed. "My brain in doing just fine, thank you for your concern. May I remind you that it got us this far. It'll get us further."

They were a fine pair, he mused. He had seen money and social prominence in her, she had seen ambition in him. He had always had political aspirations. And right now they all hinged on how far he could take Saunders and how well he could manage things. Which again hinged on getting rid of the one obstacle in his path. Harrison.

He knew Alicia was in a hurry. He deliberately paused to drain his glass, then placed it on the granite counter before slowly approaching his wife of ten years. Her glare was cutting slices all through him.

He held out his hand to show how steady it was. He could consume a great deal before it would begin to show. "See, sober as a judge," he declared.

Alicia shook her head. "That doesn't speak very well of our judicial system."

He laughed and it came out like a snort, something he knew she hated. "Very droll, my dear. Be sure to employ that rapier wit at the party."

The look Alicia gave him was cold. As cold as she was in bed. But her money and her family's social stand-

ing more than made up for any frostbite he occasion-
ally endured. If he needed pleasure, there were other av-
enues to stroll down besides gracing the silken sheets
in his wife's bedroom.

"Let's go," she snapped, turning on her heel.

With one swift movement he was in front of her,
leading the way. As it should be. "My sentiments, exactly, Alicia," he responded pleasantly.

"Not much for a night's work." Smith looked down
at the final batch of folders Jane was holding. There
looked to be no more than ten there. This was the fifth
night they'd been at this since she'd first corralled him
almost two weeks ago.

He still didn't know how she'd talked him into doing
this. When he'd initially agreed to supply the key to the
archives room in the basement, he'd assumed that it
was to be a one time thing. And then she told him that
she needed to come back—and back. He'd naturally
balked. The more often they returned, the greater the
risk of getting caught. And he had come to like this job.
Both the pay and the hours were superior to the other
jobs he'd held down recently.

But Jane had looked up at him with those eyes of
hers, the same pale, liquid green eyes that he'd fallen
for the first time around when he'd been wet behind the
ears and naive. And suddenly he'd heard himself grudgingly saying yes to her.

No, he amended now, reflecting, they weren't exactly
the same eyes. Because back then, her eyes had been
soft, gentle, beautiful. Now there was spirit in them, as

well. He supposed that probably had something to do with the cause she'd taken upon herself, to save the professor's job.

Crusading, he decided, became her.

"Sure it is," Jane contradicted. She put the folders down on an old lunchroom table that had obviously been discarded and then eventually commandeered for the basement for just such occasions. Taking out the battery-powered, pencil-thin scanner she'd brought with her, she methodically passed it over the data she needed. The information was temporarily stored in the device's memory until she could download it into her computer and print it out. "Besides, it's all in how you use what you have."

He knew what that was about. "You mean, like manipulating?"

Manipulating had a harsh sound to it, one that seemed underhanded. That wasn't her intent.

"I meant like showing things off to their best advantage. I've found that the same set of statistics can be used to back up a number of things, some even contradictory, if you know just how to apply them."

Smith stood back and watched her as she quickly uploaded the data she needed. "The professor's lucky to have you on his side."

Jane raised her eyes from her work for a second, looking at him. "I couldn't have gotten anywhere without you."

She was flattering him. Another form of manipulation? He supposed everyone was guilty of that to some degree. "You'd find a way."

She grinned. Lock picking was not exactly her forte. "I think you're giving me too much credit." Although she had to admit that it felt nice. Looking back, Drew had taken a great deal of pleasure in tearing her down every chance he could.

Scanning the last section of the last folder, she closed it and shut off the scanner. She tucked it into her purse, then picked up the folders again.

"Okay, done," she declared as she headed back to the rows of file cabinets where she'd initially retrieved the folders.

Smith, she noted, seemed determined to remain with her until the last folder was put back in its place. By now she knew it had nothing to do with his concern that something would be amiss. He was like a silent protector, she thought. She had to admit, it wasn't something she was accustomed to. And she rather liked it.

Jane paused as she tucked the last folder carefully back, chewing on an idea. An impulse, really. Shutting the drawer, she turned toward him. "Would you like to come over?"

They began walking toward the door. He kept his voice low so that it was only slightly above a whisper in case there was someone around outside. "Over where?"

She wondered if he knew how sexy he sounded. "My place."

He stopped at the door before opening it. This was completely out of the blue. "When?"

"Now. Tonight," she amended. She watched him open the door and scan the immediate area. As always, there was no one around. They'd come here after hours and, besides people from the administration building very rarely had any reason to go down to the basement. "And don't say 'why' next."

He held the door open for her as she walked out. "Why?"

Jane shut her eyes for a second, searching for patience. Maybe this was a bad idea.

No. No, it wasn't. She could sense, on some level, that he was just as much of a lost soul as she was. Except that she had Danny to anchor her and the professor to be in her corner. Smith needed to feel that there was someone in his corner, too.

"Because it drives me crazy when you say it."

She didn't understand, he thought. Quietly he led the way out. He noticed that even though she still wore heels, like the first time, she made an effort to tread on her toes so that her heels wouldn't click against the concrete.

"No, I mean, why do you want me to come over?"

Did she have to submit a list of reasons? Why was he so suspicious of everything? "Because as of approximately two weeks ago, we're partners in crime. Because we attended the same school together—"

They were out of the stairwell now and on the first floor. The lights were dimmed to save electricity. It gave the area almost an eerie aura. He wouldn't have wanted her here by herself. Just in case.

"Not for that long," he reminded her.

There were things that couldn't be measured. "I don't put a time limit on friends."

They made their way to the back entrance. Darkness and the sound of crickets greeted them as they emerged from the building. "I wasn't aware that we were friends."

Her smile was soft and it worked its way right under his skin before he realized what was happening. "We've broken into the same basement room together, I think that qualifies us as being friends."

Amusement began to whisper along the perimeter of his lips. "Strange definition."

"Strange times," she countered.

He began to walk her to where she'd parked her car, the way he had all the other times they'd gone down into the archives. She realized that Smith still hadn't answered her.

"So," she pressed, "can I interest you in some cake or some coffee?"

She'd bought a German chocolate cake from the bakery last night and had taken precautions to hide it in the back of the refrigerator, where Danny wouldn't find it. Otherwise she had no doubt he would have made short work of the dessert. The last thing she needed was to have her son bouncing off walls with a sugar high.

What she could interest him in, Smith thought, turning her words over in his head, was her. Easily.

With effort, he pushed the thought aside. There was nothing he could offer a woman. No security, no future. And someone like Jane Jackson wouldn't be interested in a man who had no future, a man who didn't even possess a college degree. Like it or not, Jane was out of his league.

Smith had every intention of calling it a night once she was inside her car. It was Friday, the end of a long, soul-numbing week. It was time for him to do what he usually did on a Friday night. Go to the local haunt in his neighborhood and wrap his hand around a beer. Or three.

The pseudo restaurant was little more than a glorified tavern, really, but it suited his purposes. The atmosphere was nonexistent, the music indistinguishable. And the best part was that he didn't have to worry about driving home under the influence. The place was close enough to walk to.

So he was more surprised than Jane when he heard himself mumbling, "Sure, why not?" to her invitation.

About to get into her vehicle, Jane laughed. She'd heard more feeling coming out of squealing tires. "Try to rein in your enthusiasm."

His eyes met hers. Whatever she wanted from him, he thought, she was going to be disappointed. He didn't have it to give. "Enthusiasm and I parted company a long time ago."

Jane didn't answer immediately. Instead he had the impression that she was studying him. "Maybe it's about time you got reacquainted," she finally said.

He was still trying to figure out what she meant by that as he pulled his car up into her driveway. She owned a house. That surprised him. Probably got it in the settlement, he decided. It was a modest single-story house. Looking at it, he saw a couple of places where it could stand a little work. A couple of the bricks leading up to the front door were either chipped or missing. And it could stand some shrubbery. Maybe even a small tree in the front yard, which was a decent size in comparison to some of the newer homes that had abbreviated driveways and no front lawns to speak of.

Jane was standing outside her open garage, right behind the car she had just pulled into the structure. The light that had gone on when the door automatically opened framed her form.

The smile she offered stirred something inside him.

He told himself he was letting his imagination run away with him. At best, this was going to be nothing more than a friendly cup of coffee. Jane probably just wanted to thank him for helping her and this was the only way she could, given her limited resources.

She wasn't even a friend, she was a co-worker, even though they were plains apart, he silently insisted.

The warm feeling in his gut wouldn't abate, wouldn't listen to reason.

"More than likely, Danny's up," she told him. Actually, she was warning him, she thought. People needed to be prepared for her four-foot ball of energy. She saw a hesitant look come over his face and wondered if he had any experience with children. If he didn't, Danny was going to be one hell of a crash course for him. "He's hyper," she admitted, "But he won't bite. That stage is passed, thank God," she added under her breath.

He heard. "Your son bit people?"

"When he was little," she quickly explained. "Not emergency-room bites, just little nips, like a teething puppy. His pediatrician said that some kids do that." The doctor hadn't elaborated as to the cause, but she had her own theory about that. By the time Danny had come along, Drew no longer made an effort to curb his tongue, his temper or his roving appetite. "I think he was just acting out because of all the tension at home. Now that 'tension' has moved to parts unknown with his girl-friend, things are a lot better."

Unlocking the door, she swung it open. The next moment her lower section was being embraced by a thin lit-tle boy whose mop of dark hair came up just past her waist.

"Where *were* you?" Danny demanded, relief, bewil-derment and accusation all mingling together in his high-pitched voice. He still managed to sound years older than he was. Jane's theory was that he had the soul of a little old man encased in the body of a five-year-old.

Jane hugged her son, then moved Danny back a lit-tle so that he could see she had brought someone with her. "I had to work late, honey."

Smith looked beyond the boy toward the other occu-pant in the room. An old woman who looked more than mildly interested as she regarded him. Her eyes were sharp as they assessed him.

This had to be the next-door neighbor Jane had told him about. Gladys, he remembered.

The woman's dark blue eyes went from him to Jane, silently conveying the question that Danny wasn't shy about asking the moment he became aware of him.

Danny's green eyes washed over him in a quick scan. "Who's he?"

Jane released the boy and stepped back. She was parallel to him, Smith noted. Deliberately? "Danny, this is my friend, Smith."

Danny's next movement surprised Smith. The boy solemnly extended his hand to him, waiting. Taking it, Smith shook the small hand gravely.

"What's your first name?" Danny wanted to know, obviously unaware that his mother had already given it to him. His eyes seemed to bore straight into him. The boy had a lot in common with his mother, Smith thought.

"Smith," Smith told him.

Danny's mobile face screwed up as he digested the information. "Funny name."

Jane looked at him, embarrassed. She'd never believed in imposing too many restrictions on her son and she'd always talked to him as if he were her equal in everything but stature. Today, it was backfiring.

"Danny."

Smith kept his eyes on the boy, pretending he hadn't heard her intervention. "I always thought so, too. 'Smith' was my mother's last name. For some reason, she didn't want to let it go, so she gave it to me. My full name's Smith Parker," he told Danny, who beamed back. It was clear he liked being treated like an adult.

"I'm Gladys Ryan," the older woman said to him, her lively eyes dancing. He had the distinct impression of being in the presence of someone who had been a force of nature in her younger years. Gladys reluctantly turned toward Jane, "And I'm also gone."

It was late and the woman had remained longer than she'd anticipated, Jane thought, walking her the short distance to the front door. "I really can't thank you enough."

"I'm the one who should be thanking you," Gladys

told her, the woman's attention still focused on the tall, good-looking man in the living room. "I love spending time with Danny. They're young for such a little while," she said wistfully. "Well, good night." She tucked her purse under her arm. "Call me anytime." Gladys looked over her shoulder at Smith, then back at Jane. "I'm available for sleep-overs, as well. Or Danny could spend the night at my place."

Jane felt warmth creeping up her face at an incredible rate. "That won't be necessary."

Gladys leaned into her. "For pity's sake, the man looks like a young Robert Redford. Don't be a disappointment to me," the woman whispered into her ear just before she left.

He tried to interpret the expression on Jane's face and failed. "What did she just say to you?"

"That she thinks you look like a young Robert Redford." There was no way she was going to tell him what else Gladys said.

Danny looked up at Smith, then at his mother. "Who's that?"

She tousled his hair, relieved to be on safe ground again. "A movie star."

He vaguely knew what that meant. Someone on TV. "Are you a movie star?" he asked Smith.

Smith looked as if he was going to choke. "He works with me at the university," she told her son.

Which brought Danny to another one of his endless questions. "You a teacher?"

She saw Smith pause and came to his rescue. "He's a maintenance engineer."

The word "engineer" had only one meaning for Danny. His eyes grew wide with anticipation. "You drive trains? Can you take me on a ride?"

She picked Danny up in her arms. "No, he doesn't, monkey, and those are enough questions for one day. Time for bed." She glanced over to the clock on the table. It was almost nine. "Way past time for bed," she pointed out.

Danny stuck out his lower lip. "But we were having fun."

She wasn't about to fall for that. "And now you're having rest."

"Aw, Mom, I wanna talk to Smith." As he made his protest, Danny turned his luminous eyes on Smith.

The similarity was striking. "He has your eyes," Smith observed.

"No. I don't. I have my eyes," Danny insisted. "See?" Danny pointed to his mother's face. "Mom's are right there."

Smith laughed and she caught herself loving the deep, rich sound. "He also has your penchant for being straightforward."

Danny frowned, lost. "What's that?"

"Something you'll find out about when you grow up," Jane promised. She turned toward the rear of the house. "Okay, cowboy, off to bed."

But Danny wasn't through yet. "Can Smith read a bedtime story to me?"

The request took Smith completely by surprise. "I, um…"

Danny's face was the epitome of innocence. "You

know how to read, right?" he asked. "'Cause I'm learning and I can help you if you want."

Smith couldn't help grinning as he looked at the boy. If only everyone was as open, as uncomplicated, as this. "How old did you say this kid was?"

"This many." Danny held up five fingers. "How old are you?"

Smith surprised her by flashing five fingers five times, then holding up four. Danny looked mystified. They hadn't gone that far with numbers yet, but she knew her son was too stubborn to let on.

"Bed, Danny," she repeated.

"But—"

"I'll read to you once you're in bed," Smith told him.

She was about to say that wasn't necessary, then thought better of it. Instead Jane turned to look at him. And then she smiled.

That warm stirring in the pit of his stomach returned, feeling more like a volcano.

Chapter Eight

Had things gone differently, Smith couldn't help thinking half an hour later as he stopped reading and looked down at Danny's sleeping face, this might have been his world. Had his life gone on the course he'd once assumed it would, he could have easily been a husband, a father reading his son to sleep.

He couldn't help feeling resentful at the cruel twist of fate that had first dangled life's small joys in front of him, putting them just out of reach, then capriciously yanked them all away by having first one thing, then another destroy his chances of attaining his goal.

First he'd been unjustly deprived of his scholarship, then when his grades had plummeted because of the depression he'd fallen into, he'd dropped out. And then, even before he could rally and talk himself into going to a city college and trying to work his way back up into a university, his father'd had a heart attack. Money was needed immediately, so he'd gone on working instead of back to school. The years just fed into one another.

And so this was now his lot.

But it could have been different.

With a sigh, Smith closed the book he had only gotten partway through and set it on the nightstand beside Danny's bed. Rising to his feet, he saw that Jane was leaning against the doorjamb, watching him with a soft, bemused expression on her face.

She looked every bit as pretty now as she had back then, he thought. Prettier.

He wasn't supposed to be thinking like that, he told himself.

Jane came into the room. Crossing to Danny's bed, she paused to tuck the covers around him and brush his hair away from his face. The boy stirred, but went on sleeping. "I never pictured you reading to a child."

He kept his voice low as he followed her back to the door. "That makes two of us."

But it really wasn't that much of a stretch, he caught himself thinking. Maybe, if things had been different, if he'd found her in that day in the dorm, or not lost his nerve…

No point in going there. Things were what they were, there was no changing them.

It occurred to Jane that there were things she had just assumed about Smith, but didn't really know. Was he married? Divorced? Was there a little boy somewhere with his face? A little girl with his hair?

She stepped into the hall. "Do you have any children of your own?"

He was standing too close to her, he realized, and took a step to the side. He shook his head. "No. I've never been married."

Jane eased her son's bedroom door shut, making sure to leave the night-light on. Danny was afraid of the dark. Just as she had been at his age. Her mother had been understanding. Just as she intended to be with Danny. "You're one up on me, then."

Which was she referring to, the child or the marriage? "What do you mean?" he asked as he walked behind her to the kitchen.

"By not being married." She frowned, trying not to think of her own fiasco. "You're better off that way. Marriage is highly overrated."

"Think so?" It was obvious by his tone that he didn't agree with her. "My parents have a great marriage. Thirty-two years and still holding hands." He hadn't gone that route because after he'd dropped out of college there had never been another girl to spark his imagination. Besides, he had nothing to offer anyone. His outlook on life was too dark these days. No woman needed or wanted that.

Jane laughed bitterly. "In the last few years of my marriage, if I was holding Drew's hands, it was to keep him from hitting me."

The second the words were out of her mouth, she regretted them. Why had she said that? She looked at Smith, trying to second-guess his reaction. He probably thought she was some kind of a loser.

What she saw on his face was surprise and disbelief. "He abused you?"

She quickly shook her head. "No. Forget I said anything." She looked around the kitchen as if she wasn't familiar with every nook, every cranny. "Look, I promised you coffee and cake—"

But Smith caught her hand before she could hurry off to the cupboard. Before she could hurry off the topic. "Did he abuse you?" he repeated.

Her fault for opening her mouth, Jane thought ruefully. She shrugged dismissively, avoiding his eyes and taking possession of her wrist. She went to the refrigerator and took out a can of ground coffee. "Drew lost his temper a lot. When he did, he tended to let his hands do his talking for him."

The one thing Smith could point to with pride was his upbringing. His own parents were generally so happy, he couldn't imagine living with the kind of turmoil Jane was describing. It had to have been terrible for her. He thought of something his mother would have suggested.

"Did you try to get him into counseling?" It wasn't anything he subscribed to, but some people did and he'd heard that it did help sometimes.

Placing a filter into the coffeemaker, she measured out grounds to make two strong cups. "Once." Running the tap water into the pot, she shook her head. "Drew charmed the counselor. That was his greatest asset—and my downfall." She poured the water in. "Drew could be very charming when he wanted to." Closing lids, she pressed the on button and water immediately began to brew. "No one believed me that he flew off the handle."

Smith watched her reach into the cupboard for two cups on the top shelf. Joining her, he moved her gently aside and took them down for her. Jane indicated the counter. He set them down.

"But if he hit you, the bruises—"

"Were always in strategic places." She traced her finger along the line formed by her shoulders. "Below the collarbone, above the knee. No one could see them unless I wore skimpy clothes. I never wore skimpy clothes," she added needlessly. "He was smart as well as charming." Taking out a container of skim milk, she shut the refrigerator again, then set the container on the counter. "Or maybe the word is calculating."

He studied her as she spoke. There was no love there when she talked about her ex-husband. Whatever had once been there was long gone. Compassion stirred within him. "Why did you stay?"

And wasn't that a question she'd asked herself, over and over again, lying awake in the dead of night? The answer was shamefully simple.

"Because I had nowhere to go. Because I was ashamed." She let out a ragged breath. "Because I thought, on some level, maybe I deserved it because things I did turned this perfectly nice man into some kind of a raving lunatic." Mind games, she thought. She'd played mind games with herself, lying, hanging on, refusing to believe it was hopeless. "So I kept hoping if I just did things right, if I didn't get him angry—"

She seemed too intelligent to buy into any of that, Smith thought. The woman he saw in front of him was spirited. Was that just an illusion? Or had she evolved because of what she'd gone through before? "How could you live like that?"

The smile that lifted the corners of her mouth in response was rueful. "Something I eventually wound up asking myself every day."

Memories, wrapped in feelings, assaulted her now. It wasn't a welcomed journey down memory lane. The coffee ceased brewing. She poured out two cups and brought both over to the table, placing them next to the milk and the sugar bowl. The cake and plate came out next. She cut slices for both of them.

"I thought, after Danny came, that things would be different with Drew. And, for a time, they were. Until the novelty wore off." Her face darkened as she remembered the fear she'd felt. "But then that temper started eating into our lives again." Her laugh was soft, tinged in disbelief. "I was almost relieved when Drew started up with a new woman shortly after Danny was six months old. At least he wasn't home."

She looked up from the inky liquid in her cup, her eyes meeting his. She expected to see pity. Instead she wasn't entirely certain what she did see. Understanding? Or was that just wishful thinking on her part? "I guess that must sound rather pathetic to you."

He took his coffee black, like she did. The milk container remained untouched. "Not my place to judge." He took a sip of the brew. It was strong and carried a punch to it. Just the way he liked it. "What made you finally get out?"

She wasn't given to lying. But to admit that she wasn't the one who left, that it was Drew who'd left her, running off with the woman he'd thought he was seeing behind her back, made her sound like a real loser. And she didn't want Smith to think of her that way. She wanted him to think of her as the woman she'd been forced to become. Strong, independent. Someone who could function on her own.

So she told Smith what she'd planned to do before Drew had done what he'd done, stealing her thunder and leaving her completely high and dry.

"Drew started yelling at Danny, really yelling at him. I knew it was just a matter of time before that escalated, before he'd start hitting him the way he did me. I just couldn't allow that to happen. It was one thing to be hit, another to watch your son being hit." She shut her eyes and shivered. The very thought of it made her ill. "Besides, it was bad for Danny to watch his mother being belittled and abused."

"Yes, it was," Smith agreed so strongly, he made her wonder if there was a story behind that.

"I didn't want him turning out like his father." That was her worst fear. "Or his mother," she added. When she saw Smith looking at her quizzically, she elaborated. "Sometimes children of victims grow up to be victims themselves…"

He thought of the boy who'd bounced into bed. At the time he'd thought he had his work cut out for him. But Danny had surprised him by dropping off to sleep within ten minutes. He guessed that bouncing took a lot out of a kid. "He seems all right to me."

Jane smiled warmly, the way she did every time she thought of Danny and how lucky she was to have him.

That was why she'd chosen to forgive Drew. Amid the hard times, the black-and-blue torso and the soul-squelching criticism, there was always that redeeming note. He had given her Danny. The child without whom her life would be horribly incomplete.

"He's more than all right," she said fondly. "He's terrific."

How much of that was exclusively because of her? Smith wondered. "How often does he see his father?"

Smith saw her square her shoulders, as if she was preparing to physically block something. "He doesn't. Neither one of us knows where Drew is and that's just fine with me." Granted, Drew needed a father figure in his life, but better no father than one like that.

Smith's mind tended to the practical. "What about alimony and child support?"

She took another sip of her coffee. She picked at the slice of cake on her plate, taking a tiny piece off the end and eating it. "What about it?"

There was something almost hypnotic about watching her eat, he thought. With effort, he dragged his eyes away. "Does he send it?"

She shook her head. It had been a year since she'd even seen a penny. But that was all right with her. She'd find a way to manage.

"Part of the fringe benefit of disappearing off the face of the earth, I guess." He looked annoyed for her. It touched her before she had a chance to disregard it. "I see it as a small price to pay for freedom."

He leaned back for a moment, as if assessing her. "So then you're all right financially?"

God, that was so far from the truth… There were times when her existence was from paycheck to paycheck. They were issued every two weeks and the few days before the money came in always felt so bleak to her.

"You know, for someone who keeps to himself, you ask an awful lot of questions." She doubted that he'd asked this many in the last six months. "Did Danny rub off on you?"

Jane was right, he was treading ground he had no right to walk on. Raising his hands in front of him in mock surrender, Smith acknowledged, "Sorry, none of my business."

No, she thought, it wasn't. But there had been a sincerity in Smith's voice that she'd felt herself responding to.

"No, I'm not." He looked at her quizzically and she forced herself to elaborate. She'd come this far, she owed him that much. She pushed on. "I'm not all right financially. If the professor loses his position, most likely, I'll be out of a job, too. That's not why I'm trying to help him stay," she added quickly, thinking he might be tempted to say something sarcastic about her dilemma. "But I'd be lying if I said that it didn't factor into it somehow."

He took the information in stride. Finishing his coffee, he set the cup aside, ignoring the cake. "You've had a rough time of it."

She didn't want pity, even if she'd earned it. Her chin raised and when she spoke, her voice was filled with pride.

"I'm doing better than most. I've got a great son and a job I like for a man I really respect and care about. The professor—and his wife while she was alive—has always been good to me." She was moving into private territory again, she warned herself. What was it about this man that made her want to share her innermost thoughts with him? She hadn't even done that with girlfriends.

Jane did a U-turn. "I'd like to return the favor and thanks to you, I've got a shot at it."

He thought of the time they'd spent together. Not exactly the kind of evenings he'd recommend for a man and a woman, but it had been strangely intimate despite the nature of their work.

"So, you're finding things to back up your claim that he goes out of his way to help struggling students." He just assumed she had since she hadn't said anything to the contrary. He'd been pulling files for her when he found that the student had taken Harrison's class, but he hadn't bothered delving into those files. That was her job.

She stopped picking at the slice on her plate and drained what was left in her cup. "For the most part."

He read between the lines. There was something more to it than she was saying. "Something wrong?"

Jane wiped her lips, then debated making another cup. Enough coffee and she'd be wired, but tomorrow was Saturday and she could sleep in—for as long as Danny would let her.

"I'm not sure. I found a couple of cases, two to be exact, where it looks as if grades on the transcript might have been altered."

Smith looked at her sharply. "What do you mean, 'altered'?"

"Just that." It made her uncomfortable to mention,

but maybe if they did talk about it, if she talked it out, she'd come up with some kind of an explanation for the change that wouldn't blacken the professor's name. Broadstreet was already trying his damnedest to do that. "In each case, a failing grade turned into a passing one."

"But not any of the professor's classes."

"That's just it. Both times it *was* a grade in the professor's class."

What worried her was that there might be more cases—and that there weren't good reasons for the changes. The first thought that sprang to mind was that the professor was accepting some sort of bribe, but that was absurd. The professor had too much integrity for that kind of thing.

Smith refused to believe it. "Can't be. When the professor was the coach, he wouldn't change any of the failing grades for some of the jocks so that they could play in the game. And there'd been pressure on him to do that," he recalled. "According to rumor, that's why Broadstreet wants to get rid of him, because he feels that Harrison was never a 'team player' so to speak. That he still believes that going to college is supposed to be about getting an education, not becoming a star athlete." He looked at her. "A man like that doesn't go around changing grades at will."

She liked his explanation a lot better than the thoughts she'd been harboring. "No, I guess not. Maybe the two I found were mistakes." She found a slim thread and began to weave it into something stronger. "He meant to enter one and he put in another by accident. Maybe he was preoccupied and when he realized his mistake, he changed them to the right grades."

"Sounds plausible." But even as he said it, Smith could see that it wasn't sitting all that well with her. "But you're not convinced."

Sitting back in her chair, she chewed on her lower lip. "I should be. I mean, if nothing else, the man is a shining beacon of integrity." She paused, blowing out a breath, a thought forming in her mind. "Even if he changed grades, I have to believe it was for a good reason. That, ultimately, it was for the good of the student somehow."

He pushed the cup back onto the table and laughed. "Well, yeah, passing instead of flunking is always a good thing for the student." He thought of himself. "If I hadn't gone into that downward spiral after losing my scholarship, I wouldn't have done so poorly in my tests. It wasn't because I didn't know the material, it was because I was depressed. I wish someone had given me a second chance to take those tests over. Getting those low grades just made me drop out before they had a chance to 'invite me to leave.'"

He watched in fascination as her eyes lit up. Did she look like that when she was aroused? he wondered. Had her husband seen her like that and still treated her the way he had? The man was a hopeless fool.

"That's it," Jane cried.

Smith pulled himself back into the conversation. "What's it?"

"Maybe that's why he changed the grades. The professor felt that the student knew the work, but there was something going on in the student's life at the time that affected their ability to concentrate, causing them not to get the grade they would have gotten had they not been facing some crisis or other."

"That's a hell of a mouthful," he commented.

Jane grew excited. The more she thought about it, the more sense it made. "When a student gets a good grade, what does that make him feel like doing?"

He thought of the people who had been in his dorm. "Going out and celebrating."

Jane waved her hand at his comment. "Besides that."

Smith grew serious. He knew how he would have responded. "Studying more to keep it up."

She pointed a finger at him. "Exactly. Maybe that was the professor's reasoning. He knew the student, knew what they were capable of and he just felt compelled to give that student that extra mental boost to see him through the bad patch."

She was whitewashing it and even though he liked the professor, he knew it wouldn't go over big with the board, especially not Broadstreet, since the president would just use it against Harrison. "It's still grade-tampering, so we can't use it."

She noticed Smith had just said "we," not "you." Her mouth curved in a smile. Whether he knew it or not, Smith had just made a giant leap over to their side. More importantly, this man who she felt was trying so hard to remain a loner had just become part of something. She didn't really know why it made her as happy as it did, but it did.

"I know. The professor's heart was and is in the right place. It always has been. But grade tampering, even for the best of reasons, would be something that the board would hold against him." Still, she reasoned, the board was made up of people, people with feelings, people who had once been students themselves. "Except maybe in the absolute sense."

"Meaning?"

"That his intention was to keep a good student from being lost." She looked at Smith, remembering what he'd gone through. "Too bad the professor didn't have a go at your grades."

"Yeah, well, my low grades were across the board. He would have had to fix all of them." He had been so devastated that someone would believe that kind of thing about him, especially without hearing him out. It completely ruined his faith in humanity. "Besides, it would have taken more than just altering a grade or two to get me on the right keel."

There was genuine interest in her eyes as she looked at him. "What would it take?"

There was no point in talking about it. "That boat has sailed."

To her, the only final thing was death. Everything else could be worked with. "Why?"

He wasn't going to answer, then decided that if he didn't, she'd probably keep after him. "I'm twenty-nine. If I go back to college, I'll be thirty-two when I graduate, assuming I could do it in three years."

She nodded her head and for a second he thought he'd convinced her. But then she asked, "And how old will you be in three years if you don't go back to college?"

She was twisting things, Smith thought, annoyed. "That's not the point."

Jane shifted in her chair, getting into his face. "That's where you're wrong. That *is* the point." She sighed, thinking of the way he'd looked whenever she'd run into him before they'd embarked on this fact-seeking mission. He'd looked embarrassed. "This isn't what you wanted to do with your life when we were in school together."

That was behind him. He'd grown up since then. "Sometimes plans don't work out."

He was still young, damn it, she thought. Suddenly she wanted to rattle his cage, to get him to go back to school and be all that he could be. "And sometimes we don't let them work out."

He banked down his temper. "How did this become about me?"

It had been about him from the moment she'd seen him reading to Danny. The sensitive soul she'd once known still existed. And he needed to know that he had people in his corner.

"Maybe the professor isn't the only one who needs saving. You have a mind, Smith, you can't just let it go to waste. Isn't there something you want to do besides what you're doing?"

"Win the Irish sweepstakes," he said flippantly.

"Something real. You're good with plants." She thought about the way he'd gravitated toward her dying weeping fig. He'd given her a report about it just today. "You said you'd brought my fig tree back from the dead."

She had no idea that she'd tread onto sensitive ground, he thought. "So I should do what, open up a flower shop?"

He made it sound foolish. She pressed on. "I don't

know. Become a landscape artist. Get a degree in horticulture." Her smile was firm around the edges. "There're probably a few things you still don't know."

"Yes, one of which is how to get you to stop meddling in my life and go back to meddling in the professor's." He was getting nowhere and he had a hunch that when it came to arguments, he was outclassed. "Look, I have to go." He pushed his chair back and rose to his feet. "Thanks for the coffee."

The moment he got to his feet, Jane stood up, as well. The napkin that had been in her lap fell like a square tan snowflake to the floor.

Reflexes had her stooping to pick it up. The same reflexes that came into play for him. Since their heads were both intent on occupying the same place at the same time, they bumped against one another. The impact jolted her so that she almost fell backward.

Smith grabbed her arm to keep her from ignobly meeting the floor with her butt and pulled her back toward him.

How, in the next moment, his lips suddenly came to be covering hers was something he had no clear recollection of.

Chapter Nine

Looking back, he should have realized that this had been a long time in coming. Maybe even for the last nine years or so. A man could fight attraction only so long. In the final analysis, impulse had just taken over. He didn't even remember initiating it.

The kiss had just happened.

And once it did, everything inside him lit up like a Fourth of July sky. For the first time in a very long while, Smith felt as if he wasn't merely drifting through the minutes of a day. It was as if something was pulling him into the light.

A little like a Hollywood version of an alien abduction, except with a lot happier results, he thought. Warmth stirred through his veins, heating him, becoming more intense by the moment.

His fingers tightened around Jane's slender shoulders. His intention had been to move her back. But he couldn't seem to get himself to act on it.

Instead he pulled her further toward him. Anchoring her to him. Strengthening the union between them until that was all there was.

The taste of her mouth, the surge of feelings suddenly running free, all evoked a hunger inside him. A hunger that had lain dormant, wasting away to almost nonexistence, for longer than he could remember.

The kiss deepened. The fire grew.

She made him feel and he didn't know if that was a good thing or a bad thing, only that he suddenly felt alive.

For just one moment he went where the kiss took him, framing her face with his hands even as Jane, by her very existence, framed the moment.

The sigh that escaped her lips went straight to his gut, tightening it.

It was real.

The attraction she'd thought she felt humming between them hadn't just been her imagination. It was real. Intoxicated, she thought she felt her head spinning as her pulse began to accelerate.

Her insides felt as if they'd been standing in the path of a hurricane. Everything had been upheaved and thrown wildly around. The feeling intensified as the kiss lengthened, strengthened. Deepened.

Jane felt herself being pulled into the very core of the kiss. On her knees, she threaded her arms around Smith's neck, her heart hammering so hard she was certain it was going to break through her chest. She'd forgotten what this felt like, being aroused. Being made to feel like a woman. Not a mother, not an assistant, but a woman in the most basic sense of the word.

And then it was over.

Cool air was rushing along her face as she tried to get her bearings. Tried to focus on something other than the fact that she wanted him to kiss her again.

Jane sank back on her heels, taking a deep breath, then letting it out. Wondering when her pulse was going to return to normal.

And then she smiled at him.

"Wow." She dragged in another breath. Her smile widened. "I must say you certainly have a unique way of helping someone pick up what they dropped."

He was watching her lips as she spoke. God help him, he wanted to do it again. Wanted to kiss her.

Wanted to have her.

Desire swirled through his belly, fanning out to his limbs. For the briefest of moments he entertained the thought of making love with her. There was nothing to stop them. Her son was sound asleep and from the looks of it, would probably remain that way. When he'd kissed Jane, he was certain he'd felt her respond to him. If he took this to the next level and further, he doubted she would protest.

Damn it, what was he thinking? He wasn't some testosterone-filled teenager. He knew his actions had consequences, even the simple ones. They weren't just isolated deeds surrounded by space and time and nothing more. If he made love to her, on some level, that was a promise, right? And he wasn't a man who made promises. Because he hadn't kept the one he'd made to himself a long time ago. To become something.

This above all else, to thine own self be true. Well, he hadn't been true to himself, so he couldn't be true to anyone else and this was just playing with fire, damn it.

Getting a grip on himself, Smith rose. Once up, he extended his hand to her. As she wrapped her fingers around his and pulled herself up, he found himself struggling against longing again.

This had to stop.

"Sorry," he mumbled.

On her feet, she stared at Smith for a moment, wondering if she'd misheard him. "There's nothing to apologize for."

This was virgin territory for him. She'd invited him over for coffee and cake, not something more personal. "Then you didn't mind?"

She had no way of knowing that her smile was going straight into his gut.

"Mind being made to feel human? No, it was rather nice to remember that I am." She couldn't help thinking how different Smith was from Drew.

But Drew was different from Drew when you first met him, a small, cautionary voice inside her head whispered.

She knew she had to step back. It was better to be safe than sorry. Wasn't it?

But she wasn't all that sure just how enticing being safe was. Smith's kiss had woken things inside her, things that had once been very precious to her. She had to admit that she liked the way it felt. Had missed the way it felt.

Taking another breath, she tried to make light of what

had just happened. Even if things inside her weren't behaving that way. "You kissed me, Smith. You didn't drag me off into a back alley and rip off my clothes. There's nothing to be sorry about."

He didn't know about that. At least from his end. Because kissing her had really stirred up something inside him. And although he wasn't a novice when it came to the male-female thing, he wasn't sure just how to deal with what he was feeling.

Reaching out, he touched her face, the thought of kissing her again lobbying for his full attention. He almost gave in. But he knew if he did, it wouldn't end here or in her living room. And he wasn't ready to go anywhere else. Literally and figuratively,

Smith dropped his hand to his side, shoving it into his pocket. "I'd better go."

She didn't want him to. Which meant that he had to. Because she didn't trust herself. He'd made her feel wonderful and vulnerable all at the same time. She wanted to curl up in his arms even as she knew she should be holding him at arm's length.

Or maybe it was herself she should be holding at arm's length.

This was *not* the time to get sidetracked. She was fighting to help the professor keep his job. So that she could keep hers, as well. She needed a clear head for that. And right now, her head was as clear as a muddy stream and getting cloudier by the second.

Pressing her lips together, she nodded at the wisdom behind his words, grateful he wasn't one of those men who jumped to take advantage of a situation.

"Maybe you'd better," she agreed in a husky voice she barely recognized as belonging to her.

She walked him to the door on legs that were less than stable. "Thanks for everything." Then, because she realized how that sounded, she added, "Reading to Danny, helping with the files…" Damn it, she was babbling. You would have thought she'd never been kissed before. "I'll see you Monday," she said, cutting herself off before she became a total idiot.

Desire made another impromptu appearance, grabbing hold of him and refusing to be dislodged. He could feel it pulling him toward her. Smith stood his ground, knowing it was best for both of them.

Even so, he wanted to kiss Jane again in the worst way.

And that's just exactly the way it would have been, he told himself. The worst way. So instead of brushing his lips against hers, he pulled his head back abruptly without making any contact at all.

Nodding, he mumbled, "Right," and was on his way before he could change his mind again or do something that in his estimation would be stupid once it was held up to the light of day.

Closing the door, Jane leaned against it. Waiting for her insides to stop vibrating like a plateful of gelatin in an earthquake.

What the hell had that been all about? She upbraided herself.

The chilling realization that all her defenses had gone into systematic meltdown frightened her beyond words. Sure, she'd been attracted to Smith when they were in school together. Back then she'd hoped, in vain, that he would ask her out. But she was barely out of her teens then and very naive. She knew better now.

Where had this wealth of passion come from?

Stupid, her inner voice jeered. *It comes from not having been with a man for so long, you can hardly remember what it was like.* And whatever else Drew might have been, she remembered, he'd been a very good lover. In the beginning.

Beginnings were wonderful, she thought, moving away from the door and out of her shoes. But they were swiftly followed by events that were not so wonderful, Jane reminded herself, moving her shoes out of the way. Their marriage had only been a couple of months old when Drew began turning her into an emotional prisoner, dangling lovemaking as a prize in front of her.

Because she'd hungered for the next time that he would be loving, the next time he'd be tender, she would deliberately block out all the bad times. She was far from proud of herself. Back then, she'd find herself trading everything she was forced to endure just for those isolated, golden moments when he was good to her.

As time went on and Drew became more secure in his dominant role, those moments became fewer and further between.

No man burned brightly in the dark, she told herself. As she moved through the room, she began picking up toys that Danny had left behind in his wake, tossing them into the toy box that resided, close to empty, against the side wall.

No, no man burned brightly, she thought again. And

that included someone like Smith, who had given up on the world and himself.

She paused, catching her reflection in the window. "And if you think you can save him…" she said to the woman looking back at her. "Get over it, Janie. You're not some crusader from the Middle Ages. You can't save everyone. Saving the professor's job is more than enough of an assignment for you."

Bending to pick up a couple of Matchbox racers, she deposited those into the toy box, too. Her body was still tingling, she thought. Just went to show you how a little could go a long way.

It also showed her that there wasn't going to be any rest for her in the near future. She might as well make herself useful, she decided.

With a sigh, she went to retrieve the pencil scanner from her purse. If she couldn't rest, she might as well download the information she'd scanned from the latest bunch of files she'd found.

The needle on the speedometer was beginning to establish a relationship with the number fifty. It was a thirty-mile zone. Biting off a ripe curse, Smith eased back on the gas pedal. Normally he was a very careful driver, but there was nothing normal about the way he was feeling right now.

He glanced in his review mirror to make certain he hadn't attracted the attention of any nearby policeman. But there appeared to be none in sight. Relieved, he blew out a breath, warning himself that he might not be so lucky the next time. He had to get back on an even keel.

Jane had aroused more than his body tonight, he thought. There was something about being around her, about being exposed to her spirit, that had coaxed hope out of the vault where it had been residing all these nine years. And it dragged out old, cobwebbed thoughts about returning to school.

He thought about it on occasion, but never seriously. But one thing after another always seemed to come up, getting in the way, until the thought about returning to get his degree eventually died a quiet, unobserved death. Jane, with her blunt question, had yanked the funeral shroud right off it. Forcing him to reexamine the idea.

Making him want to do something with his life besides get through the day for the first time in he couldn't remember how long.

A few stiff drinks would chase those ideas away, he told himself as he drove along a main thoroughfare. But even as he toyed with the notion of anesthetizing his brain, the thought occurred to him that maybe, just maybe, he didn't want the idea to be chased away. Maybe he *did* want to go back to college to get his degree. Okay, he was twenty-nine. But he was also never going to be any younger than he was right now, today. And twenty-nine wasn't exactly having one foot in the grave.

The idea was worth examining.

Later.

Right now he needed to purge this evening from his mind. Because to think about it was only going to lead to frustration and he'd already had enough of that in his life to accommodate two people.

* * *

"Doorbell!"

Danny sang out the word the next morning just before noon, his young voice drowning out the episode of "Marvin and His Friends" that he was watching for the umpteenth time. As bright and gifted as Danny was, he seemed to take huge comfort in watching things over and over again until they both had the words committed to memory. Jane supposed that was what they meant by brainwashing.

Trained by default, Jane immediately stopped what she was working on at the dining room table. On her feet, she was instantly engaged in a foot race with her son, each intent on reaching the front door first.

He was supposed to have outgrown this by now, not become more of an opponent, she thought grudgingly. "Danny, what did I tell you about not opening the door to strangers?"

He never dropped a step. "I won't know if it's a stranger until I open the door."

There was no arguing with the logic behind that one, she thought, torn between frustration and pride at his ability to reason on this level, given his age. She was convinced that his intelligence was nature's way of making his hyperactivity bearable.

Because her legs were longer than his enthusiasm, she managed to get to the door first and to place her hand over the doorknob. But Danny had been a close second.

"You are just way too smart for my own good, Danny," she informed him with a sigh. But she wasn't about to concede the war to him. This was her son's safety she was concerned about. "Okay, from now on, just don't open the door to anyone."

His interest in whoever was on the other side of the door already waning, Danny looked at her with wide, discerning eyes that fronted a mind that was always working.

"Not even you?"

She figured that was a safe enough bet. Someone could be pretending to be her to gain access. Gladys certainly couldn't outrun him the way she had. "No, not even me."

She could almost see the wheels turning as he shot back, "What if you lose your key?"

Jane rolled her eyes, knowing that if she answered that question, there'd be another one right behind it and another one after that. She was way too tired for this kind of thing today. Sleep last night had been elusive, coming only in fitful dribbles and drabs. There was no two ways about it. What had happened between her and Smith last night had really shaken her.

More than that, her own reaction to everything had thrown her for a loop. Because she found herself lying awake last night, thinking about him. Wanting him.

Wasn't going to happen, she promised herself. She was definitely not emotionally ready for that.

"We'll talk later," she told Danny, her hand still on the doorknob.

"I'd appreciate that," a deep voice on the other side of the door commented. It sounded strained.

It also sounded familiar.

Looking through the peephole, she saw only foliage. Foliage that sounded a great deal like Smith.

Or was that just her imagination, intent on driving her crazy?

"Are you planning to open the door anytime in the next decade?" the tree asked.

That was definitely Smith. Her heart made an upward pass into her throat and took up residence there, throbbing double-time.

Unlocking the door, Jane quickly swung it open, only to come face-to-branch with her formerly mortally ill fig tree.

"Benny?"

"No, Mom, it's Smith," Danny announced gleefully, already out the door. Impatient, he'd gone to see the back of the talking tree for himself. His disappointment at discovering that there was a person holding it had abated when he realized that it was the man who had read to him last night. Most grown-ups tended to ignore him after giving him a pasted-on smile.

Stunned, Jane stared at the tree. Smith was the last person she'd expected to see here today. He'd certainly left quickly enough last night.

She pulled herself together, remembering that he was supposed to return the plant to her office. Wasn't he? "Um, why did you bring Benny here?"

"Who's Benny?" Danny asked.

Smith moved his head to the side, looking around the tree branches until he saw the boy. "Your mother named the tree," he told Danny before shifting it over to the side.

Perplexed, Danny's brow shriveled until his small,

dark eyebrows pulled together and merged over his perfect little nose. "Why?"

Smith looked from the son to the mother. "My question exactly."

Jane shrugged. "It looked as if it needed a name." Actually she named everything, her car included. When things had names, it generated a more homey feel and she was desperate for that. She focused back on the tree and tried not to think about the man who had brought it. "Why did you bring him here?"

Smith had been all set to bring the tree back to her on Monday before he'd decided against it. "Because I didn't just bring him—" My God, he thought, she had him doing it, giving the tree gender; he consoled himself by saying he was just doing it for her benefit, "—back from the dead to see him die again. Besides, I saw your yard last night." He nodded toward the interior of the house and the yard that lay just beyond. "You could stand to have a few trees planted back there. It's too barren right now."

"So's my office," she pointed out, although she had to admit, the tree had taken up a lot of room in a place that didn't have that much to spare.

Smith remained adamant. "An office is no place for a tree. You want something green, get a plant."

Okay, he was obviously the specialist. "Any recommendations?"

Smith was about rattle off the names of a few plants that did very well indoors, then remembered who he was taking to. The woman who claimed she unintentionally committed genocide when it came to anything housed in a pot. The selection automatically narrowed.

"For you," he finally said, "I'd suggest getting a cactus."

Humor quirked her mouth. His hold around the base of the pot tightened. "Why, because I'm prickly?"

"No, because for the most part, cacti are hearty—as long as you don't overwater them," he cautioned. More than a few drops at a time tended to cause a great many of the species to rot.

She laughed. She had a tendency to go exactly the opposite. "No problem with that, I usually forget to water plants."

He remembered the fig tree's bone-dry soil. "I had a hunch."

They were still standing on her doorstep. She was aware of Danny shifting from foot to foot beside her as she regarded the tree Smith was holding.

Last night, you were the one he was holding.

She banished the thought as she touched one of the leaves. There were new green shoots all over the tree. "So you think I should plant this in my backyard?"

"No, I think *I* should plant this in your backyard," Smith contradicted. He nodded toward the car he'd parked in her driveway. "I brought a shovel, fertilizer, specially mixed dirt. Shouldn't take too long," he told her, in case she was going somewhere.

Pleasure slid through him when she shrugged carelessly and said, "Time doesn't matter, unless you're in a hurry to get somewhere."

He'd remained quiet long enough. Danny tugged on Smith's shirttail. "Can I help?" Eagerness brimmed in his high voice.

She laughed. "Last chance to say you're on a schedule, otherwise…" She looked from him to her son, her implication clear. Danny had a way of eating up any schedule.

"No, no schedule." He looked at the boy. "So, you want to help, huh?"

Danny bobbed his head up and down like one of those toys he remembered seeing looking back at him from the rear of a car window. Smith paused for a moment, thinking. He was accustomed to working on his own but the boy looked so eager, he didn't want to shut him out.

"Okay, we'll find something for you to do." Slight like his mother, Danny didn't look strong enough to dig. "Why don't you go and open up the side gate for me so I can get Benny here—" he slanted a glance toward Jane as he referred to the weeping fig by the ridiculous name she'd christened it "—into the backyard without having to go through the house."

"Okay!" Danny cried, happy to be of service. The next moment he was plowing through the house and then tearing out through the rear sliding-glass door.

Smith shifted the tree for a better hold. "Doesn't he ever walk?"

Jane shook her head. "Not that I ever noticed." And then she smiled warmly at him. The quickest way to her heart was to do something nice for Danny. "This is very nice of you, you know."

Smith shrugged. He wasn't very good with gratitude of any kind. "Well, I said I'd try to bring your tree back from the dead."

She'd fully expected him to keep his word. He was that kind of a man. "No, I mean letting Danny help. You realize that it's probably going to take you twice as long to get it into the ground than you anticipated, don't you?"

His experience with children was almost nonexistent, but he'd extrapolated before coming over this morning. "Yeah, well, I kind of worked that into the schedule," he told her.

He sounded so serious about it, she couldn't help grinning. "I always thought that you were a fast learner, Smith."

He looked at her to see if she was pulling his leg or not. He couldn't make up his mind. "That was a long time ago," he muttered as he began to walk off toward the side yard.

"It's like riding a bicycle," she called after him. "You never forget how."

When he looked over his shoulder at her, he noticed that she was running her fingertips over her lips. Was she remembering last night?

As if suddenly aware of what she was doing, Jane abruptly dropped her hand to her side and went back into the house.

"Yeah," he repeated to himself just before the side gate swung open. "You never forget how."

Chapter Ten

"Isn't it a little late in the season to be planting a tree?"

Jane asked the question as she set the tray she'd brought out to the backyard on the small, redwood patio table. It was just big enough to seat three. Closely.

Smith and Danny had been at this for a while now. True to his word, Smith had brought everything that was needed to make sure the tree had a healthy head start. This included several bags of nutrient-rich soil that now lay completely depleted to the side. He'd used the contents to line the hole he'd dug.

Danny made a beeline for the tall glass of lemonade and the extra-large, fifteen-minute-old, chocolate-chip cookies that were piled up on the plate like a warm, chewy pyramid. Smith remained where he was, stopping to lean on the shovel he'd been using. He mopped his brow, catching his breath.

He wasn't the only one in need of oxygen.

The day was moderately warm, but not uncomfortable. Unless you were digging in the yard. Smith had taken off his shirt and his body was glistening now with a fine layer of perspiration.

Jane felt the inside of her mouth turning into something rivaling the chemical composition of freshly packaged cotton. She'd already figured out that he wasn't out of shape, but she had no idea that Smith was nearly as well built as he actually was. His upper torso was toned and pleasingly muscular, without an ounce of excess fat anywhere. He might have allowed his future to go to pot, but no such criticism could be applied to the state of his body.

It was obvious that he'd treated it like a temple. She couldn't help wondering how many women had come to worship there.

Suddenly realizing that she hadn't breathed for several seconds, Jane dragged air into her lungs. It didn't subdue the rhythm of her erratic pulse. The last time she'd looked out the window to see how Smith and Danny were faring and if her son had driven the man to distraction yet, making him throw down his shovel as well as his resolve, Smith had had his shirt on. Granted it was unbuttoned with the ends teasingly moving in what little breeze there was, but it still covered more than it didn't.

That wasn't the case now and there was a world of difference seeing him like this. The man looked like a body building commercial come to life.

The same arousal she'd experienced last night came back to haunt her with a vengeance, capturing her body and holding it prisoner. Reminding her that it had been a very long time since she'd been truly intimate with a man. Not since long before Drew had finally left.

"It might bear watching," Smith allowed, answering her question about the tree. "But as long as there isn't a cold snap before it's established, it should be all right—barring subzero weather." Which didn't happen very often around here. And weeping figs were fine down to twenty-five degree weather.

She forced herself to look past his magnificent torso and at the tree in question. "What happens if there's a cold snap?"

Taking his handkerchief from his back pocket, he wiped his forehead. "If there's one before it's established, the tree might die. After it's established, the leaves'll drop off and it could die back a little for a while, but eventually it'll come around."

"A fighter. I like that."

Jane gave her full attention to the tree for a moment. It certainly looked a lot healthier than it had in her office. There was no doubt that Smith knew what he was doing. He was wasted working at the school in his present capacity, she thought. It was obvious to her that he loved plants. At the very least, he should be running his own nursery.

Her eyes shifted to his. "Wouldn't it be warmer for Benny if he was closer to the house?" She remembered reading that somewhere.

Smith had planted the tree at the other end of the yard,

near the fence. Resting the shovel against it, he shook his head. "Not unless you want your pipes compromised."

She stared at him. She was pretty sure he wasn't sending her some kind of a veiled message. He wasn't the type to resort to innuendoes. Besides, Danny was here, eagerly hanging on to every word out of his mouth. She instinctively knew that Smith would never say anything around a child that wasn't completely G-rated.

"My pipes?"

"Tree roots seek out water," he explained. "The ficus is particularly aggressive when it needs water." Smith stuck the handkerchief back into his pocket. "You, by your own admission, have a penchant not to water things. If the tree is too close to the house, it might take matters into its own hands and go through your water pipes."

Danny was clearly hooked by the scenario. "Wow, just like in a scary movie."

She looked at him sharply. "What scary movie?" She wanted to know. He was strictly forbidden to watch any if he came across one on TV. With his vivid imagination, any ninety-minute horror movie would translate into six to nine months of nightmares. For both of them.

Danny was the soul of innocence as he looked up at his mother, his third cookie in his hand. Slender shoulders beneath a blue-and-white striped shirt rose and fell in an exaggerated fashion.

"I dunno. A movie about scary trees, I guess." The next second, he was focused on Smith again, a brand-new idea bursting across his fertile, overactive brain. "You could come here and water the tree for Mom if she forgets."

Jane slipped an arm around her son's shoulders, trying hard to reconstruct her knees at the same time. Smith had put down the shovel and was heading toward the patio. And her.

And looking sexier and more mouth-watering with every step he took.

"I'm sure Mr. Parker has more important things to do than to come by here and water the tree for us every day, Danny."

"It doesn't need to be watered every day," Smith told her matter-of-factly just before picking up the glass of lemonade. He downed it in one long swig, much to the unabashed admiration of the boy looking up at him. If Smith was a hero before, he'd just been elevated to the position of a superhero.

Admiration was shining in his green eyes. "Wow. And you didn't burp or anything."

"Danny!" There were times she wished her budding genius wasn't given to blurting out whatever came into his head.

Danny didn't see the problem. "Well, he didn't," he protested.

She decided that it was safer to turn her attention back to what Smith had just said. "It doesn't need to be watered every day?"

"No, just two or three times a week. Deeply."

She couldn't quite picture what he was saying. Maybe because she was trying too hard to ignore the fact that Smith and his smooth, bare chest was standing much too close for her to be able to string together coherent thoughts that ran into more than a few words.

"Deeply?"

"For a long time." He poured a little more lemonade from the pitcher into his glass. His biceps rippled. Her mouth grew dryer.

"I'll show you when I'm finished," Smith volunteered.

Danny moved his never-still body between them, facing Smith. "When we get done here, I'll show you my cool new video game," he promised.

When Smith didn't respond immediately, she came to his rescue. Danny had a habit of presuming too much. "Honey, Mr. Parker's doing us a favor. I'm sure he's got other things to do once he finishes planting Benny." Which, from the looks of it, was very soon, she thought. A wave of sadness washed over her out of nowhere.

It was, Smith thought, the perfect out. And, under normal circumstances, he would have bet even money that he would have taken it.

But that was before he'd arrived. Before he'd started working. Before his guard had somehow mysteriously eroded and he'd allowed this effervescent kid to get to him. Danny was every bit as hyper as Jane had warned him the boy would be. Danny was also extremely intelligent. A few times during the conversation this afternoon, he'd actually forgotten that he was talking to a five-year-old. The boy thought and spoke with a maturity beyond his years. Rather than get irritated at the frequent questions and interruptions, Smith had found himself intrigued.

Still, no one was more surprised than he when he looked in Jane's direction and told her, "Actually, I don't."

Danny literally jumped up and down as he cried, "Great!"

Jane said nothing because she was speechless. And pleased.

And afraid to be pleased.

Danny had taken to Smith like wildfire to dry grass. Ever since Drew had walked out of their lives, she knew the boy had been hungry for male companionship.

That made two of them, she thought ruefully. Except that she would have never believed it of herself until last night. She'd been so terribly disillusioned by her marriage, so disappointed in herself because of everything that had happened, everything that she had *allowed* to happen, that she had been firmly convinced she was going to be one of those women who'd tried marriage once, decided it wasn't for her and then spent the rest of her life devoted to her child and her career.

Except that her career, such as it was, was in jeopardy and her son was currently enamored with a man who looked as if his body could have been used as a model for sculptures of Greek gods. The really mouthwatering, hunky ones.

Careful. There are minefields out where you're walking.

She had to remember that, Jane silently upbraided herself. And most of all, she had to remember that absolutely nothing was ever as good as it seemed, as good as it promised to be.

His kiss was.

Jane slapped down the thought. She'd been tired last

night. Tired and vulnerable. Both were factors that easily lowered her resistance and more than clouded her judgment. She was willing to bet that if Smith kissed her again today, she wouldn't react the same way.

A sliver of excitement shimmied up and down her spine just thinking about putting her theory to the test.

"These are good," Smith remarked as he picked up his second jumbo cookie and bit into it.

Being around Jane brought out his sweet tooth, he thought. Ordinarily he had no desire for desserts, preferring fruit to something that resorted to sugar and flour for its sweetness. But these cookies just melted in his mouth.

They made him think of her.

Danny puffed up his chest proudly. "Mom makes the best cookies," he said in his best "buddy" voice.

Smith raised his brow. "You made them?" That would account for why they felt as if they were warm. He'd thought it was his imagination.

She nodded, feeling suddenly embarrassed. "Can't you tell by the irregular shape?"

Smith frowned as he looked at her. "You shouldn't do that."

Jane instantly stiffened. Criticism always made her remember Drew. His sharp tongue had slashed through first her confidence, then her self-esteem, until she'd had neither.

Her eyes darkened as she raised her chin defiantly. "Do what?"

Something was going on here he wasn't following, Smith thought. But it didn't keep him from making his point. "Point out the defects in everything you do. Especially when they're so minor."

His eyes held hers for a moment. Someone had done a number on her, he thought. Most likely that scum of an ex-husband of hers. He felt a surge of regret that the man had dropped out of sight. Someone needed to teach him a lesson about acceptable behavior.

"I like funny shapes," Danny offered loyally, grabbing up another cookie. His fourth by her count. Where did that boy put them? She was convinced they turned into pure energy the second they went into his mouth.

"See?" Smith said, as if that made his point. The soft smile on his lips filtered into her, chasing away her wariness.

Laughing, she tousled Danny's hair. Rather than pull away, Smith saw the boy lean into her, as if silently showing the world and him that they were a unit. The boy reminded him a little of himself at that age. He'd been a great deal quieter and not nearly as intelligent, but he'd felt that same sort of bond with his mother.

Nostalgia whispered over him as he remembered a far more innocent time in his life. A time when he'd had dreams. And hope.

Smith nodded toward Danny. "You know that's going to change, don't you?" he said to Jane. When she looked at him quizzically, he elaborated. "There's going to come a point when he won't know you, at least when his friends are around."

She nodded. It was a common enough occurrence. Gladys had already commented on that rather wistfully the other day, recalling the behavior of her own two sons. Mercifully, for most it was a passing phase. She didn't know what she would do if she ever became permanently estranged from Danny.

Jane gave Danny a quick hug, which he absorbed, then wiggled out of because they weren't alone. She dropped her arms to her sides. Maybe it was starting already, she thought with a tinge of sadness.

"So I've been told," she acknowledged. "I'm savoring every moment I can."

Which was true. She never took affection of any kind for granted, having done without it for so long. Maybe that was why she had been such a perfect prey for Drew. Without a family, she was starved for contact. The professor and his wife had been wonderful, but they hadn't taken the place of someone of her own.

Neither had Drew, after a while.

"Besides, Danny's just five," she pointed out. "I think I've got four or five years to go."

Danny momentarily slid onto a chair beside the table, taking the glass with both hands and trying to drain it the way Smith had drained his, she noted. A clear case of hero worship already. Was she making a mistake, allowing this to happen?

"How old were you before you started ignoring your mother?" she asked.

He saw that Danny had set down the glass and was listening intently. "I didn't. But then, I was the exception. I didn't go along with the norm."

"I noticed that about you." The words had come out of her mouth before she'd thought to stop them. She cleared her throat, embarrassed and completely without a lifeline. "Well, I'd better go back inside." Opening the sliding-glass door, she stopped and looked at him. Not certain if she was making another mistake or not. "You're welcome to stay for lunch. I'm making pot roast—"

"For lunch?" Most people had sandwiches or something light. Unless they were hosting Sunday dinner for the family the way his parents sometimes had.

"It's 'cause it's my favorite," Danny explained before his mother could. The boy's wide green eyes pinned him to the spot, putting refusal on the same plane as ripping the wings off butterflies. "You'll like it. Mom sticks a bunch of little potatoes around it. They look like marbles, but they don't roll too good," Danny confided.

"Too well," Jane automatically corrected. Her voice didn't even penetrate the aura of hero worship wrapped around her son. Danny was staring up at Smith with huge, hopeful green eyes.

"Then I won't roll them," Smith replied.

Danny laughed. It was a joyous, infectious sound that seeped into his bones as he listened, warming them, Smith noted. Like mother, like son.

"Then you'll stay?" Jane asked. "For lunch," she tacked on to avoid misunderstanding, then thought she sounded like some kind of awkward, social misfit who had trouble forming complete sentences.

"Yeah, I'll stay." His eyes met hers for a split second before he turned his attention back to his work. In that brief encounter, enough electricity was generated to light up Las Vegas for a month.

"Yippee," Danny cried, sounding, for once, just like a typical five-year-old.

Yippee, Jane echoed silently, watching Smith as he walked back to the tree.

She just barely managed to catch her sigh at the last moment before it escaped and convicted her of the felony of being a drooling idiot.

Damn, but the man looked good coming *and* going.

It took more than several beats of her overworked pulse before she could rouse herself properly and walk back into the house.

She had a pot roast to make. Provided she hadn't forgotten how to cook altogether.

For some reason the good deed he'd convinced himself was the only reason he was here in the first place had somehow managed to turn into an all-day affair. One thing just kept leading into another.

The weeping fig had long since been placed into the ground. It had been fertilized and watered a little after one.

Lunch was supposed to be the cut-off point. He'd told himself that he would just have a few bites and then make an excuse and leave.

It was hard taking only a few bites. She made pot roast the same way she made cookies. It melted on his tongue before he could chew. He found himself going back for seconds, something he rarely did.

And after lunch, his escape had been foiled because he didn't feel like escaping. Instead he'd felt full, mellow and because of that, he'd been pliable. He offered no resistance to Danny when the boy took him by the hand and dragged him to the small family room.

Jane told him that this was "Danny's second room," and he could see how it could be construed that way. It was the perfect place for the boy to play. The newest game system stood waiting to be put into play. More than a few video games were stacked beside the twenty-seven-inch TV set.

"You play video games?" The way the boy asked, it was obvious that he meant it as a rhetorical question. Everyone in Danny's world played video games. Even his mother.

"No."

Danny couldn't have looked at him in more stunned surprise than if he'd just said that he was actually from another galaxy, far, far away. Had his eyes been opened any wider, he would have been in danger of having them fall out.

"Never?"

"Nope, never." Smith shook his head to confirm the words, thinking that would be the end of it.

He hadn't counted on Danny's tenacity. The boy had flashed the thousand-watt smile he had inherited from his mother and confidentially announced, "Okay, I'll teach you. Nothin' to it."

And then he proceeded to do just that. With patience that was years beyond his chronological age, Danny quietly explained the rules and demonstrated a dexterity that Smith found impressive.

Not to mention infectious.

Smith wound up playing not one, but all of the new

games in Danny's arsenal. And enjoying himself in the bargain. He'd convinced himself that winning didn't matter—until he'd actually won a round and discovered a very pleased surge traveling through him.

"Lucky accident," Danny had crowed. "Can't happen again."

And they were off again.

The afternoon slipped away into early evening and with evening came another meal invitation.

Looking at his watch while at the table, Smith realized that he had spent most of the day here. Like a member of the family.

He couldn't remember when he'd enjoyed himself half as much. Or at all, now that he thought about it. Since his father had opted for an early retirement because of his heart condition and his parents had moved to Florida, he was alone most of the time.

This felt better.

As before, they cleared away the table in unison, with Danny assuring him that they had to do it or else "Mom gets mad."

"Can't have that," he'd agreed, catching Jane's eye. Catching her smile, as well.

Finished, Danny pivoted on his heel to face Smith. He knew that begging for a few more hours wasn't going to get him anywhere, so he decided to work within the framework of the system.

By ambushing Smith. "Can you read to me again?"

The man had been more than patient. It was time to cut him loose, she thought. Besides, she could see that even in this short amount of time, Danny was getting incredibly used to Smith. If the man decided not to be friendly anymore, her son would be devastated. It wasn't good to promote this any further than it had already gone.

"Honey, we've eaten up Mr. Parker's whole day," she pointed out tactfully. She never got any further in her argument.

Danny was raising his sunny face up to Smith's. "But you had fun, right, Smith?" he asked with all the confidence she hadn't felt in a long, long time.

"Yes—" Smith raised his eyes from Danny's beaming face and looked at her, his deep voice rumbling along her skin "—I had fun."

Where was this wave of excitement, of anticipation, coming from? Smith was talking about the day he'd spent with her son. And now he was leaving. There was no reason for what was going on in the pit of her stomach, no reason at all.

It didn't stop.

"But now he has to go," she said to Danny.

Smith looked at her. "Are you throwing me out?"

His tone was so serious, it took her back for a second. And then she pulled herself together. "No, I'm giving you a way out."

He didn't answer her. Instead he looked at Danny's eager face. There was no way he could turn the boy down and not feel like a heel. That wouldn't have been a good way to cap off a very enjoyable day.

He put his arm around Danny's slim shoulders. "What do you want to read tonight? You know, you fell asleep before I finished reading the book you gave me last night."

"I was just resting my eyes," Danny corrected, using the excuse his mother used every time he accused her of falling asleep while watching one of his favorite video tapes that revolved around the misadventures of a boy and his invisible best friend.

Smith did his best to look contrite. "Oh. Sorry."

There was clearly amusement on the man's lips, Jane thought. It was hard for her not to react. Though she told herself that this was just one evening, one day out of a lifetime, that there was no way she could allow herself to think of it in any other way, she could still feel herself melting.

More than just a little.

But then, she thought not for the first time, the quickest way to her heart had always been through Danny.

Chapter Eleven

She knew the second that he returned to the room. Maybe because as she'd moved around first the kitchen, then the living room, straightening up, she kept watching for Smith to enter.

Jane tossed the two action figures she'd just picked up into the toy box. It took effort not to cross to him, but she didn't want Smith to feel as though she was crowding him.

"Danny asleep?"

The door was on his right. If he were smart, Smith thought, he'd start inching his way toward it. But instead, he found himself walking into the living room. And to her.

"Yeah."

That warm feeling that kept reoccurring each time

she looked at him today opened up in the center of her chest again. Spreading. She had to concentrate to keep it from overwhelming her.

"You know, he's really taken with you."

Smith read between the lines. "And you don't want him to be."

She didn't want him thinking that she wasn't grateful for the way he was with Danny. For the patience he'd displayed. "I didn't say that."

He shook his head. "You didn't have to. I can see it in your eyes."

This time, she did cross to him. Maybe too close for her own good, but she wanted to make him understand her concern without offending him.

"That's confusion," she corrected. "Danny's got a big heart. I don't want to see him hurt."

"Hurt?" The last thing he'd want to do was something that would make the boy unhappy.

She pressed her lips together and nodded, forcing herself to look him in the eye when she said it. She'd been far too timid all her life and she was determined not to be now.

"When you stop coming around."

"'When,'" Smith repeated the word slowly, as if it had width and breath. "So for you it's already a foregone conclusion?"

She raised her eyes to his. "Isn't it?"

Until this morning, he'd probably have said yes. The pattern of his life was to keep a distance between himself and the world that had disappointed him so badly.

But now, he wasn't so sure about that pattern. His

eyes slipped along her face and he caught himself thinking that she was beautiful, even without makeup.

"Why don't we just take it one day at a time?" He smiled at her. "No reason to anticipate a flood when there isn't even any rain in the sky."

Her mouth twisted in a smile. "But it doesn't hurt to carry an umbrella." She took a breath. "Danny took his father's disappearing act very hard. He has a huge capacity to love someone and at his age, he's still eager to give his heart to someone else… Someone like you, because you take the time to talk to him. To be his buddy…" She knew that kind of thing couldn't continue. And when it stopped, it was Danny who'd be hurt. And maybe her, as well. She raised her chin. "Well, I just want to make sure he's not going to get hurt."

His eyes held hers. He couldn't make promises, because promises tied you down and he wanted to remain free. And yet…

And yet he was happy today. As happy as he could remember being in a very long time. "There aren't any guarantees in life."

She looked away and began to pick up toys again. Or tried to. "I know, but—"

Bending, he got to the toy before she did. They both had a piece of it. "Are we talking about Danny or you?"

She was forced to look at him. "What?" Stiffening, she straightened, letting him bring up the toy. Taking it from him, she tossed it over to the box. "Danny, of course."

He nodded, but he had a suspicion that he was right. That the fear of being hurt didn't just include her son, but her, as well. And why not? The jerk she'd married had done a number on her. Anyone who'd ever gotten burned was leery about picking up matches again. He knew that firsthand.

"I'll do my best not to hurt him." And then, as he looked at her, Smith brushed his knuckles ever so lightly along her cheek. He saw her pupils widen. "It's the best I can offer."

It felt as if her breath was standing still in her throat, threatening to become solid. That same scrambling of her pulse was starting. "I guess I can't ask for any more than your best."

He didn't want to talk, didn't want to think. Not about consequences of actions, not about tomorrow, or even the next moment. Only now. Only this woman who was making him forget to stay distant. His own code of self-preservation against disappointment, against the world, was disintegrating. And all because of a wisp of a woman who barely came up to his shoulder.

If he had an ounce of sense in him, Smith upbraided himself, he'd turn on his heel and make his exit. Leave while the leaving was good.

But it wasn't good. Not anymore. The only thing that was good was standing right here in this room in front of him.

Unable to help himself, Smith framed her face with his hands, tilting it up just a little. And then he kissed her. Softly at first, then with growing intensity.

Wanting only to savor the taste of her mouth, silently swearing to himself that it was only going to be for a moment.

But he lied.

He didn't just want to savor the taste of her mouth, he wanted to savor her. All of her. Longing traveled through him like hot syrup, covering everything.

His hands left her face and went around her waist, pulling her closer to him than a whispered prayer. As he felt her body pressing against him, a fire ignited within him. It was as if he'd just tossed a lighted match into a gasoline can.

Jane was kissing him back. Not softly, not gently or timidly, but with passion.

Excitement roared through his veins, a fire line rushing from its source. Anticipation filled him even as his head began to swim. Badly.

Another minute and he knew he wasn't going to be able to navigate at all. Wasn't going to be responsible for his actions.

With superhuman effort, he pulled himself back. His gut twisted as he forced the words from his lips. "Jane, maybe I'd better leave."

From out of nowhere, panic skittered through her on tiny rodent feet. He was changing his mind.

But the look on his face didn't belong to a man who'd had a sudden change of heart and was making a dive for freedom.

"Do you want to?"

"Want to?" he echoed. There wasn't anything in this world he wanted less. "Oh God, no."

Relief rushed over her like a cool wind on a hot day. "Then don't," she murmured, pressing her lips to his.

She was as hungry as he was. Hungry because a part

of her desperately needed to feel that she was still attractive, that Drew's constant straying from their marriage bed meant that there was something wrong with him, not with her.

That she wasn't lacking, only he was.

By the very touch of his hand, Smith made her feel desirable. Made her feel beautiful.

Heaven help her, she wanted him to remain, to make love with her until she couldn't think straight.

Jane caught his lower lip between her teeth, gently playing with it. Trying her best to bring his desire to the forefront.

And succeeding beautifully.

She was making him crazy. He was fairly frantic for the feel of her.

Unable to stay in check any longer, Smith allowed his hands to roam along her body. As she melted against him, a fever pitch began to rise within him, swiftly taking him to the point of no return.

And this time, she was the one to pull back, her breasts heaving as she tried to drag in air to steady herself, or at least her voice.

His eyes searched her face, looking for a sign of withdrawal, a sign that she felt she was making a mistake. Something felt crushed within him, but he couldn't force himself on her, no matter how much every part of his body begged him to.

It took a second before he found his voice. "I'll go," he told her.

"You try and you won't make it to the door," she warned, her body almost trembling from the want of him.

He didn't understand. "Then what?"

Her heart pounding, she laced her fingers through his, tugging him in the direction of her bedroom. She was almost out of her head with desire, but not so much that she'd left the mother she was behind.

"If he gets up for some reason, I don't want Danny getting an advanced education."

Smith was chagrined. Jane was right. He'd forgotten about the boy. But he didn't normally think in terms of children. And right now, he wasn't thinking at all, only feeling. Strange, overwhelming feelings that filled up every inch of space inside of him.

And then, within a heartbeat, they were in her room. Jane closed the door behind her and turned toward him. Her meaning crystal clear. There was nothing in their way any longer.

He'd been watching the hem of her light blue tank top, skimming along her waist, hinting at the firm skin beneath, all day and it had been driving him crazy every single second of that time.

Reaching for the hem now, he pulled it up over her head, tossing it to the side. There was no bra beneath, just as he'd suspected. Only perfect breasts, each a handful. He filled his hands, holding her. Letting lightning zip through him. Fighting the urge to bring his mouth down where his thumbs were.

He had time. They had time. He had to remember that.

The next moment, his eyes on hers, he stripped off his own shirt, tossing it down to hers.

And then they sealed together, heartbeat to heartbeat. His lips raced over hers as he kissed her with a mind-numbing force. A vortex seemed to open up around him, pulling him in. He went gladly, without resistance. And all the while, his hands kept taking possession of her, claiming bits and pieces until he had all of her.

Oh God, what was she doing? She was the one who could put a stop to this. He'd given her two chances, offered to back away. She should have taken him up on it at least once.

But the problem was, she didn't want to back away. She wanted this to happen. Every fiber of her body wanted this to happen. Quickly. Before common sense found a way to intervene, to make her act as sensibly as she'd been raised to behave.

But she was sick of acting sensibly. Sick of feeling alone. Yes, there was Danny, and being his mother was supposed to be enough. And most of the time, it was. But there was no denying that there was this opening, this ache, that she couldn't ignore. Not always.

Not now.

With eager, almost-fumbling hands, she unnotched Smith's belt, opening it, then undoing the button to his jeans. Everything inside of her was trembling as she dragged in her breath and pushed the jeans down his hips. She pulled his small, black briefs down with it.

So intent was she on what she was doing, on the way his mouth heated against hers, Jane didn't realize that Smith was doing the same thing with the denim shorts she'd had on. She felt the snap just below her belly button release, felt the metal zipper glide down along her abdomen as it parted. Felt the shorts slide down her legs.

She stepped out of them automatically, as if that was the next move her body was programmed to follow.

Her thong underwear was missing in action, tangled with her shorts.

And then their bodies were both as nude as the day they had entered the world. Except now they were both pulsating, both anticipating what was to come.

She could feel desire and longing radiating from her core to every part of her body. Jolts of electricity struck as Smith passed his hands not possessively but almost reverently over her. The jolts increased sharply as his lips trailed along her limbs, her throat, her belly. More than just minor earthquakes began erupting everywhere he touched her.

Everywhere he pressed his lips.

As his tongue teased where his lips had passed, she could feel the eruptions coming to a head. Clustering faster and faster.

Tiny orgasms mushroomed, gathering their force together for a major explosion.

Her breathing grew erratic. She did her best to regain at least a foothold back into her own territory. Before she couldn't focus at all.

Raising her head, she kissed the side of Smith's neck, then his throat, working her way over to the other side. His heavy breathing empowered her, sending strength where just a moment ago there'd been almost a draining weakness humming through her limbs.

But the next second he'd recaptured his ground. Flipping her around, he pressed her back against the mattress. She felt herself drowning in a sea of desire as the palm of his hand pressed low against her belly and his fingers sought her out. Teasing her as they lightly skimmed along the outline of the very center of her. More explosions threatened to send her over the brink, into complete euphoria.

And then he was entering her, causing hot, moist crescendos to build. She eagerly wrapped her legs around his torso.

Their hips locked in a timeless dance that took them higher up the summit until the very moment when the fireworks went off, lighting up the sky. Continuing until desire momentarily spent itself.

The descent back to earth and reality was both sweet and painful. Jane could hardly pull in enough air to keep from passing out.

With a heavy reluctance, she felt herself reentering the world she'd temporarily left behind. She lay there, waiting for disappointment, for guilt to come and ruin what had just happened. Waited for the oppressive sensation of a blanket smothering her last whiff of joy.

Neither disappointment nor guilt came. Whatever else might occur to her later, or happen tomorrow, she knew in her heart that this was good. More than that, that it was perfect.

Drenched in an unshakable contentment, Jane sighed as the world slowly came back into focus.

Smith shifted his weight off Jane, forcing himself to look at her face. Fully expecting to find some sort of recrimination there. After all, he hadn't set out for this to happen. He'd just meant to leave her be, to go home. He was certain that she'd expected the same.

This had far surpassed expectations, a small voice inside his head whispered.

There was no hint of regret on her face. But maybe she was masking it. He had to ask, he needed to know. "Are you all right?"

It took her a second to find enough air to answer without gasping at the end of her sentence.

"I've never been so all right in my life." And then her own words echoed back to her. Would he misconstrue what she meant? "Or was that the wrong thing to say?"

Relief was staking out a claim on the same area concern had inhabited only moments ago. "Why?"

She had no other way to frame this but honestly. She'd never gained a proficiency in playing the games that couples played with one another. She always said what was in her heart. "Because that might make you feel that I'm eager."

He laughed, an odd sort of peace, a tenderness he wasn't accustomed to experiencing, washing over him. It felt good. "I don't think you gave anything away just then."

"No strings," she said suddenly, afraid that he might think she was trying to ensnare him. She wasn't sure what she was doing, being here like this with him, but snaring him in some kind of emotional trap wasn't part of it.

He regarded her curiously. "Are we talking about Pinocchio's lifelong ambition or something else?"

Was he making fun of her? "No, I meant between you and me. No strings."

He paused for a moment, studying her face. Trying to sort things out. Trying not to give in to the well of desire that had suddenly materialized again. "Are you asking me or telling me?"

"Telling." Asking him if he wanted no strings would have sounded needy and she didn't want to come across any more vulnerable than she felt certain she already did. Than she already was.

Was she telling him that she was an independent woman, one who wasn't about to be tied down by any silent or implied promise? Or was she voicing this because she thought he wanted to hear it? If it was the latter, it put her one above him because right now he didn't know *what* he wanted.

Other than her again.

"Are you saying that for my benefit?"

She evaded the word yes. "Isn't that what men want to hear?"

He could feel a smile teasing the corners of his mouth. Until he'd begun interacting with Jane, he hadn't felt like smiling at all. Now he could feel one forming from the inside out. "I haven't taken a poll lately."

He was making fun of her. "Smith—"

"Jane," he countered, his raised voice cutting her short. "What?"

His arm pulled her closer. His naked body pressed against her. She could feel his desire for her growing. "I want to kiss you again. Do you think I could do that without it having to come up for some sort of a referendum?"

A smile formed at her very center, spreading out to all parts of her, dragging sunshine with it. "I think that could be arranged."

"Good." His voice dropped low, husky. Thrilling her. "Because I really want to kiss you again."

And he did.

Over and over again, until his desire was at an even greater height than it had been the first time.

As was, he noted, hers.

They both made love with an abandonment that was new to them. And gratifying. He explored her body as if he hadn't just brushed his fingers along every inch of her, as if his mouth hadn't explored the most sensuous parts and committed it all to memory. Over and over again, he made her his willing prisoner and discovered that he was the same with her. And that, at least for the night, the invisible shackles he bore didn't bother him.

It struck him with some force and not a little surprise that after it was over and she lay in his arms, spent but incredibly peaceful, that he found himself even more reluctant to leave. That he wanted to stay.

This was an entirely new situation for him. Up through high school, he'd been too intent on reaching goals, on getting to where he was going, to devote much time to dating. The girls who had been in and out of his life had been pretty much interchangeable. He was hard pressed to remember the right names with the right faces.

The same could be said about his first year at Saunders. He really didn't even remember dating. And once he'd left the university, he'd lost all interest in finding anything beyond a night's worth of pleasure, if that much. Marriage or even some kind of long-term relationship never crossed his mind. Because of what had happened to him, he firmly believed that he had nothing to offer a decent woman, no future. So he went out of his way not to become involved with women he might have eventually felt attracted to.

All that seemed in the past now.

Remorse raised its head. He'd messed things up, royally. He knew that.

But the thing of it was, he didn't care. All he cared about was Jane.

Was that so wrong?

His feelings in flux, he clamped down on them, refusing to go any further. Holding Jane to him as they lay in bed, the sheets tangled around them, he kissed the top of her head and drew the moment to him. Knowing it would fade all too soon.

"So, how's the investigation going?"

She was surprised he wanted to talk. Drew had always just rolled over onto his side and gone to sleep, leaving her, satisfied or not, on her own.

But this isn't Drew, it's Smith.

Impulsively, Jane pressed a quick kiss to his chest, taking comfort in the warmth that radiated against her lips.

"Slowly. I'm just not finding enough files that have to do with the professor." And this could turn into a very long, tedious process. The one thing they didn't have that much of was time. "Any ideas?"

Smith began to shake his head, then stopped, realizing that he might have a solution to it after all. "You know, Harrison has this room he goes to."

Instantly alert, Jane lifted her head, her hair raining

down along his chest as she leaned forward over him. "A room?"

"It's right by the stairwell. I saw him go there a couple of weeks ago—it was the day we had that run-in about the ladder."

A slight shade of pink rose up her cheek. "Yes, I remember. Go on."

Smith thought back to the day he'd observed Harrison. "He had files in his hands and he was looking a little jumpy. Then he disappeared into that room for a while. I'm guessing he left the files there—and that whatever files you find there might belong to the students who had the most interaction with Harrison."

What he was saying made sense, even though it seemed almost underhanded of the professor to be hiding files. But then, how aboveboard was she, snooping through the archives, trying to unearth ammunition to help them shoot down Broadstreet's efforts to dislodge the professor? she asked herself.

One way or the other, the undeclared file room bore looking into. "Okay, we need to look there."

He played devil's advocate, mindful that he was doing it with a woman who was more than eager to view the material. "What if you come up with something that winds up backing Broadstreet's position?"

Broadstreet thought of the professor as an outdated failure. Her mind went instantly to the grades that had been changed. For the purpose of their study, those files weren't going to see the light of day. "Not going to happen."

He pressed. "But what if—?"

"Then we leave it buried," she declared heatedly, forgetting the very naked, vulnerable position she was in for a second. "I'm not looking to earn a Boy Scout badge here, I'm looking to keep the professor in his job."

"Girl Scout," he corrected.

She was so wound up, he caught her off guard. "What?

"You said Boy Scout," he said innocently as he cupped one of her breasts, slowly massaging it, "you meant Girl Scout."

She struggled to keep her mind focused. "Are you grading me for content?"

"Grading you?" Smith laughed, the sound embracing her as he shook his head. "Lady, you've gone off the Richter scale. I *can't* grade you."

Her smile softened her features, making her look the way she had in class a long time ago. "You know, you're very nice."

He knew people who would argue with her assessment. His mouth quirked in the semblance of a smile. "Haven't been accused of that for a long time."

She touched his face, making him look at her. "Doesn't have to be said for it to be true."

He felt her shift against him, then press a kiss to his throat. Desire flared instantly. He looked into her eyes. "You're up to doing this again? Now?" he asked incredulously.

Her smile was warm and went straight into the heart of him. "I'm up to it. If you like. It's been a long dry spell for me."

"I definitely like," he said just before his mouth came down over hers again.

Chapter Twelve

Gilbert looked up from the ream of official memos the chancellor always felt necessary to release at the beginning of each school year. Rocking back in the leather chair that bore the imprint of his body, he listened for a few minutes without speaking to the uplifting sound that filled his office.

It was the little things in life, Gilbert thought, that were always the most precious. Finally he felt as if he had to comment.

"You're whistling, Mr. Parker."

The sound stopped abruptly.

He'd let his mind drift, Smith thought. He kept his back to the professor as he tested his handiwork. The window sash moved with ease and the annoying squeak was gone.

"I guess I am," he admitted to the windowsill. "Didn't mean to disturb you."

"On the contrary," Gilbert was quick to interject, "I like to hear people whistling. Or humming. In my experience, people who do either are generally happy."

Smith turned from the window slowly. He didn't like anyone delving into his life, even marginally. The professor's eyes met his. Smith was about to deliver a toneless denial, then pulled back and reassessed his automatic response. It didn't ring true, even to him. He *was* happy. Happier than he could remember being, even though he'd tried to put in safeguards against this kind of thing happening.

Not that he didn't want to be happy, just that he'd come to realize that the feeling usually carried a toll with it. It was the adage, *What goes up, must come down.* Conversely, if he progressed on an even keel, if he didn't allow himself to rise to the heights, then there would be no depths to tumble into. Disappointment wouldn't place a choke-hold on him and drag him down because he had nowhere to be dragged down from.

Except that now he did.

And try as he might, Smith couldn't manage to squelch his feelings. It was like attempting to fit a foam pillow into the palm of his hand. Some part of the pillow always managed to squeeze out through either the top or the bottom of his fingers.

"I heard Jane humming today," the professor offered innocently. Smith looked up at him sharply. "Must be looking forward to the fall semester." There was nothing in his expression to give the slightest hint at what he was thinking. If he was somehow linking the two of them together. "I always liked the start of a brand-new year," he confided. "Everything's so fresh, everything's so new. The possibilities seem endless."

And then he paused. Gilbert couldn't help wondering if he was going to be allowed to remain at Saunders to see the year to its conclusion. The uneasiness in his bones warned him not to set too large a hope on that happening.

He supposed he really shouldn't complain. He'd been a rich man up until now. A good woman at his side, a wealth of students to help guide along the paths they'd chosen. Doing what he could to make the journey easier for the ones who showed promise and dedication. What more could a man ask for?

It was just that he didn't know what he was going to do with himself if he would no longer be allowed to come to the university every day.

He pictured having one long, endless vacation stretching out in front of him. The thought chilled him. Vacations were all well and good if they were finite, with a goal attached to them, be it seeing places or just rejuvenating. And then getting back to work.

It was the work that was important to him, the work that made the difference between just existing or accomplishing something. If his position was taken away from him, he knew he'd lose all sense of purpose.

He was a teacher as much as he was a man. It was just something that was ingrained into his soul. Something that defined him, just like having blue-gray eyes or having brown.

A cough came into the midst of his thoughts. Smith

was clearing his throat. Embarrassed, Gilbert realized that he'd allowed his mind to drift again. He supposed anxiety did that kind of thing to you. Made time stand still as it whisked you off into some vortex where only you and your fears existed.

He gave Smith his full attention now. "I'm sorry, what did you say?"

"I said I was done, Professor." Smith gestured toward the window, which he'd left closed. "Unless you had something else you'd like me to do."

Rising from his desk, Gilbert walked over to the window, circumventing Smith's large frame. His hand on the sash, he opened it with ease. Ninety percent of the windows on the campus didn't open. They belonged to buildings that were far newer than the one they were presently in. This was one of the old buildings. One of the first to be built on the property. Money always seemed to be tight, although, he thought, there always seemed to be enough for the sports teams and the athletes they were attempting to lure to Saunders. But the upshot was that no one had thought to upgrade the windows here and seal them in.

He liked it that way. Liked being able to open a window at will. It allowed the spring breeze in, helped temper the summer heat and let him feel the approach of autumn just by standing by his open window.

"Excellent," Gilbert pronounced, turning from the window. He smiled at Smith. "As always. Thank you, Mr. Parker."

"Sure."

Smith picked up the ends of his toolbox and brought them together before closing the lid on it and snapping the lock. Nothing more had been needed than an application of WD-40 and a little pressure delivered via a screwdriver.

The professor could have easily done it himself, he mused. Unlike so many of the other instructors at Saunders, the professor was always a gentleman, no matter what was going on in his life. It wasn't right what the board was trying to do to him, Smith thought.

A sense of indignation stirred in his chest now the way it hadn't before. He hoped Jane and whoever else she'd enlisted in this crusade of hers could find a way to save the old man's job. He deserved it.

About to leave, Smith paused in the doorway, looking back at the man who was still standing beside the window, his hands clasped behind him as he looked out on the campus.

"For what it's worth, Professor, I think Saunders could use a few more 'old-fashioned' teachers like you." He deliberately used the term that Broadstreet had used to condemn Harrison.

Gilbert smiled his gratitude. "It's worth a great deal to me, Mr. Parker. A great deal."

With a nod of his head, Smith left, closing the door behind him. In his breast pocket was a list of things he still had left to do today. There was enough to keep him busy until day's end even if he moved fairly quickly.

But after he left the professor's office, Smith paused in the hall and looked toward Jane's door. Indecision gave way to decision. He knocked on her door before reason prevailed and he talked himself out of it.

The moment he knocked, he heard papers being shuffled on the other side of the door. A drawer closed before she said, "Yes?"

Smith suppressed a smile. Her work had obviously taken a back seat to her crusade. The woman had passion. Lord, did she have passion, he thought, remembering the other night. He would have never thought, in his wildest musings, that there was so much fire beneath the surface.

It's always the quiet ones. Wasn't that something his father used to say? As always, his father was dead on.

Smith eased the door opened and poked his head into the office. "Hi."

Not expecting him until much later, Jane felt herself brightening immediately. Her face felt as if it was splitting open as she grinned. "Hi."

There was no real reason for him to stop by like this. Except that he wanted to. "I was wondering if we were on for tonight. The basement," he added in case she thought he was referring to something more intimate. Because part of him was but for the life of him, he wasn't sure how to go forward.

Jane's been humming.

The professor's words replayed themselves in his head, empowering him even though he wasn't quite sure just *what* was going on.

Jane could feel herself growing warm just looking at him. Heat spread from her fingers, her toes, the top of her head.

C'mon, Jane, you're a grown woman with a kid. You're not a teenager anymore.

But heaven knew she felt like one. Felt as if everything old was suddenly brand-new and fresh again. It was as if she was seeing the world for the first time. Everything before now was a blur.

In her heart, she knew she was just setting herself up for a fall, but she couldn't help it. A very small part of her was a hopeless optimist. Even though Drew had done his best to kill her spirit, he hadn't managed to completely destroy the optimist that dwelled inside of her.

Rising from her chair, Jane motioned Smith into the room, then closed the door behind him. The small "click" registered in her brain. They were isolated from the world. With effort, Jane banked down the urge to throw herself into his arms and kiss him.

If she did that, it would be all over. The man would think he was dealing with a crazy woman, she cautioned herself.

"What's up?" he asked.

Me, for one, she thought. But she tried hard to sound practical, as if she'd had a reason for asking him in other than just wanting to look at him. Other than just wanting to feel her pulse race.

"I've been thinking about that room you told me about last week. The one by the stairs." She'd looked at it earlier, had tried the doorknob, but it wouldn't give. As she knew it wouldn't. "How can we get into it?"

She'd already mentioned it to Sandra Westport, and to Rachel James, another one of the professor's former students who was outraged by what was happening and had volunteered to help. Both thought that it might be a good idea to investigate whatever the professor had in that room. All three of them were hoping they might come across something powerful enough to make their case for them, or rather, for the professor. They were in silent agreement that, more than likely, the professor would never use the full arsenal at his disposal if he felt that it might somehow reflect badly on one of his students.

The man was far too altruistic for his own good, Jane thought. But she wasn't encumbered by any such motives. All she wanted to do was to save the professor's job. And her own in the bargain.

Smith paused, thinking. Mentally he went over all the keys on his ring. "I'm not sure if I was ever given a key to that."

"Oh." She began to cast about for ways to get around that.

"But we can still get into it."

Her eyes widened. She should have known he'd come through for her. The man had a great deal to recommend himself. "How?"

The less she knew, Smith thought, the better. If someone was going to get into trouble over this, it should be him. He waved away her question. "Just leave that up to me."

There was no hiding the admiration in her voice. "I guess you're even more resourceful than I thought you were."

Smith stood over her for a moment, imagining taking her into his arms, imagining bringing his mouth down to hers. He told his imagination to go take a cold shower. "You'd be surprised."

Her eyes washed over his slowly, coming to rest on his face. Making him feel as if he'd just been touched in all the places that counted.

"I like surprises," she told him, her voice low. "Good ones."

"I'll see what I can do. I'll be back later," he promised. Then, just before he left, impulse seized him. Taking hold of her shoulders, Smith brushed his lips against hers and left her staring after him, trying to still her erratic heartbeat.

Man, oh man, she was in trouble. Big time, Jane thought. If she had an ounce of sense, she'd run for cover. But ounces of sense, she knew, were next to impossible to come by.

He thought about telling her when he returned a little after six that night, then decided that the end of the evening might be more appropriate.

Right now, she had things on her mind.

They both did.

Unable to find a key to the small storage room that apparently no one seemed to even be aware of except for the professor, Smith had used skills he'd picked up from an old private investigator who had taken a liking to him when he'd done a few odd jobs for him several years ago.

Acting as his lookout, Jane couldn't help glancing over toward Smith and taking in what he was doing. It looked as if it was straight out of a movie.

"So if I ever need someone to help me break into a place after hours, I guess that you'd be the man to go see."

Smith made no intelligible answer, merely grunted as the lock finally gave. He put the two thin pieces of metal he'd used into his back pocket, then tried the doorknob. It turned easily.

Checking once more to see if the coast was still clear, they slipped into the storage room quickly.

The impressed look on Jane's face was not lost on him. The woman made him feel as if he was ten feet tall and bulletproof and while he knew he wasn't, the feeling was something he still savored.

Smith flipped on the overhead light as he closed the door behind them.

The room was small, crammed and smelled even more musty than the room where the archives were kept in the administration building. There was also less illumination to be had, since there were no windows to the outside world and just one lone light bulb of medium wattage hanging overhead.

An old discarded desk was against one wall, taking up a great deal of the space. Beside that, vying for floor space, was a single file cabinet. It was butted up against makeshift shelves that were filled to overflowing with worn textbooks.

At first glance, the textbooks seemed to deal exclusively with English literature, but upon closer examination, there were several handbooks devoted to coaching football lodged there, as well. On the very top shelf were a handful of video tapes, all apparently concerning themselves with outstanding play-by-play moves of victorious games the professor had coached.

She'd all but forgotten about that, Jane thought. The professor had not only taught English, but had once been the football and then baseball coach, as well. And, if Broadstreet had his way, the man wouldn't even be an academic adviser any longer.

Jane swiftly surveyed the area. "If I was a borderline claustrophobic, I'd be sweating bullets right now." As it was, the air felt stale as she took it into her lungs. Only a few minutes in and the room was already beginning to feel very warm.

"At least there aren't rows and rows of file cabinets filled with folders to go through," Smith commented, looking at one lone file cabinet.

Jane tried to open the first drawer and found that she couldn't. She jiggled it again and the drawer held fast. "There might not be any at all if you can't find a way to open this cabinet." She frowned. Why would the cabinet be locked? What could the professor have in here? She caught her lower lip between her teeth, looking at him hopefully. "Do those things you just used work on this?"

"Can't hurt to give it a try," he said gamely, taking them out again.

It wasn't easy, but Smith finally managed to get the file cabinet open.

Eager to get started, Jane still looked at her partner in crime with stunned admiration. "I guess the world is just lucky that you didn't decide to embark on a life of crime."

Pocketing his tools a second time, he looked at her significantly. "Until I hooked up with you, I always walked the straight and narrow."

This really bothered him, she thought, being under-handed even for a good cause. She could admire a man like that. Smith had an incredible amount of things going for him. He just *had* to go back to school to get his diploma. She just knew he'd feel better about himself once that was out of the way.

"And so you will again," she promised. "Once we get what we need." Opening the first drawer, she looked into it. It was filled to capacity with files. "This is more like it," she enthused. "I don't have to keep sifting through files after files, looking for the professor's students." She flipped through the names, recognizing several at first glance. "These look like there're all his."

It was late. The professor hadn't left until seven tonight because the new semester was almost upon them and he was busy getting ready. Trying to keep, she knew, a positive outlook.

Jane stifled a yawn she hadn't realized was there until it tried to slip through her lips. She was more tired than she wanted to let on.

"You know, I'm tempted to just take a few of these files home with me. A few at a time," she repeated, underscoring how easy it would be. "I mean, how's he going to notice? Some of these files don't look as if he's touched them for a while. Look at this dust." She moved some aside with her fingertips for his benefit.

"Who are you trying to convince, you or me?"

He caught that, she thought, but then, she would have expected him to. The man was sharp. "Me, I guess. And even if the professor does see they're missing, how's he going to know that we were the ones who took them? There's no surveillance camera here."

To his thinking, there was a much easier way around all this. "Wouldn't it just be simpler if you told the professor what you were doing? Get his input?"

She shook her head. It was much more complicated than that. "For all his warmth and kindness, I never quite know how to read the professor. He might say no and once he does, my hands would be tied. I couldn't just go against him."

But Smith grinned. If she thought he believed that, she was as naive as she looked. "I sincerely doubt that. I would have believed it a few weeks ago, but now, seeing you in action, I get the feeling that you'd do whatever you felt was right, whatever it took, regardless of who told you not to."

Smith was right, she realized. She wasn't quite the mouse she'd been when Sandra had first approached her about doing this. She didn't know if it was the crusade to save the professor's job, or being with Smith that empowered her this way. And she wasn't about to examine it because some things should just be left alone and enjoyed, she thought. The moment you began to question things, to dissect them, they changed. And she didn't want that.

"I'll take that as a compliment."

"That's how it was intended." With the desk on one side and the cabinet on the other, there was very little space to move for one person, let alone two. Their bodies were right up against one another and he could feel that his wasn't about to remain dormant for long. "You know," he told her, his breath moving along her upturned face, "I don't ordinarily like aggressive women. But in your case, I'll make an exception."

"Good," she deadpanned, "because I'd hate to have to wield my power over you."

He liked her like this, relaxed, teasing. Liked himself this way, as well. It was all new to him. "Think you're tough?"

Like a bantam fighter, she raised her chin, teasing him. "Yeah."

"You're not," he told her, running his hands along her bare arms. "You're soft." Even in the dim light, he could see desire rising in her eyes. The same desire he felt inside of him. "Very, very soft."

"So are you," she said in a voice that was barely above a whisper. "Inside all that bravado, you're soft, sensitive."

The next moment, all the good deeds and noble intentions that had entered the room with her moved over, taking a back seat to this newly polished desire that seemed to be with her every single waking moment of the day. As well as having worked its way into her dreams.

All she could think about was the next time she'd be in his arms.

Like now.

The kiss exploded between them. Their lips were all but fused together, draining and nourishing one another all at the same time.

Her pulse racing, she paused to catch her breath. Leaning her forehead against his chest, Jane sighed deeply.

"We're behaving like a couple of schoolkids."

"About time, too," he murmured, tilting her head back and kissing her again. And again. And with each time, the urgency he felt for her swelled and grew. "I've had this fantasy about you almost from the first time I saw you."

She wasn't quite sure what he was driving at. Wasn't

even reasonably sure her name was Jane. "About making love in a cramped supply room?"

She felt the warm huff of air as he laughed. The sound surrounded her. Making her feel safe. She knew she shouldn't cling to that, but she needed to. Something about measuring a second in heaven against an eternity in hell crossed her mind. She pushed that aside, too.

Nothing mattered except this second.

He threaded his fingers through her hair, toying with it before he pushed it back. "About making love with you all over the campus. In the library, in the cafeteria, in a lecture hall."

It sounded wonderful. "If we sold tickets, we'd be rich."

He shook his head. "Nope. No tickets. I don't want to share you with anyone." Looking at her, he flashed a momentary grin. "Not even for show and tell."

"That's good, because I'm a very private person." She unhooked the snap on his jeans as she said it.

The next moment, her mouth was back against his.

Chapter Thirteen

The lovemaking was as exquisite as it was frantic.

Rather than build, it erupted like spontaneous combustion with each of them desperately wanting to experience that ultimate rush that they knew was waiting for them within the other's arms. They hurried, afraid that the next moment might rob them of something precious, might deprive them of something they needed as much as the very air they breathed.

Rather than a slow strip, clothing was swiftly pushed up, or down, as long as it was gotten out of the way. Each kiss became more powerful, more demanding than the last. Hands raced for touch, for feel, for possession, each movement fueling the next.

Smith pulled the ends of her blouse from her skirt so quickly, in the back of his mind he was afraid he might have torn the material. His hands delved beneath the soft material and her bra as the need to mold his fingers around her breasts all but savaged him.

Jane sucked in her breath the moment she felt his hands on her body. It came in short, shallow gasps. Her mouth still sealed to his, she felt herself first lifted then pressed down against a hard surface. The next moment, Smith had pushed aside the pile of books that had been stacked on the aged desk and positioned himself up, over her.

She shivered as she felt the heat of his desire press down hard against her body. Jane arched her hips, moving against Smith. Driving them both into a fever pitch.

With one swift snap of his wrists, like a magician he removed her underwear. She arched higher, grabbed at his shoulders, holding on for dear life.

The joining was urgent, as was the silent melody drumming through their veins, its tempo ever increasing. Moving to its demanding beat, they drove each other over the top. The climax was jolting, hard and all-encompassing.

For a few moments there was nothing but the sound of their breathing, raspy and short, within the small, closet-like room. He wasn't sure just how long they remained that way, only that he could have gone on listening to her breathe indefinitely. Maybe forever.

And then Smith forced himself to focus. Getting up on one elbow, he looked at Jane, at her face. He'd managed to erase most of her makeup. She was more beautiful than ever. A tenderness filled him even as surprise stood off on the sidelines. He wasn't accustomed to fielding these kinds of emotions.

All of this had really been a first for him. He'd never given in to his emotions like this before. Never felt about a woman the way he did about Jane. What was that line from that movie? Something about her making him want to be a better man than he was, that was it. And that was what having Jane in his life did for him. He wanted to be a better man. Because of her.

Smith looked at the scarred oak surface they'd just christened and a slow smile spread across his lips. "This is probably the most activity this desk has seen in a long while."

A laugh escaped her lips. Jane feathered her fingertips along his mouth. He had the most wonderful smile, she thought. It completely transformed his face from that of a loner to be leery of to someone who was sweet, kind, approachable. She could feel her heart swell. The careful, baby steps she'd warned herself about taking were a thing of the past.

And she was running to the light.

To warm herself in the aura of his smile. She looked over his head, toward the bookshelf. "I may never look at *Crime and Punishment* the same way."

He was only vaguely aware that it was a novel set in Russia and about several hundred pages too long. *"Crime and Punishment?"*

She laughed and pointed to the bookshelves. The professor owned three different-looking copies of same book, one taller than the rest, another fatter. Each was put out by different publishers. They were standing side by side just in her line of vision.

"It was the last thing I saw before the world caught

on fire." She knew it wasn't the kind of thing to admit to a man, but she had never been the type to play games. She wasn't about to begin now. And she wanted him to know that.

Leaning over her, Smith brushed a quick kiss against her lips, knowing anything more would make him linger and want to begin all over again. Being with her was like suddenly finding out he was capable of doing magic—because he was in the presence of magic.

How could her husband have walked away from someone like her? Smith wondered. He supposed he shouldn't question that, just be glad it had happened. Because if Jane were still married, if she were still attached to that lowlife she referred to as her ex-husband, she would have never been here, with him, like this.

Getting off the desk, he pulled up the zipper to his jeans, then extended his hand to Jane. When she locked her fingers around it, he helped her to her feet.

Still feeling more than a little dazed, Jane cleared her throat, wishing she could clear her mind as easily. Realizing what she had to look like after the whirlwind tryst, she adjusted her clothing and ran her fingers through her hair.

And then embarrassment caught up to her. She glanced at the naked desktop. Part of her was surprised it wasn't charred in places. They had gone at it pretty intensely.

"I've never done anything like that before," she confessed.

Needlessly from his standpoint, he thought. Smith found himself intuitively knowing more things about

Jane than he'd ever known about anyone else. She would have been the last person he would have thought of as making love in a storage closet. Or any other outlandish place for that matter.

"Me, either," he responded. She looked a little surprised by his admission. "I'd thought about it," he added, "but I've never done it."

Men made love in all sorts of places. Once, to taunt her, Drew had hurled a whole list of unorthodox places he'd made love to women who weren't her.

"Why?"

A lot of men bragged and said all sorts of things they felt enhanced their image. He didn't belong to that club. "Because you weren't available."

She could feel herself melting like hot candle wax. For a moment she hugged his words to her. "Lord, but you do know your way around a line."

"No," he told her, his eyes on hers, "I don't."

And she believed him.

The temptation to kiss him again was all but overwhelming. She struggled against it and won. For the moment. Otherwise they'd be in here all night and nothing would be accomplished beyond acquiring a tremendous rosy glow.

"We'd better get to work," she murmured, turning away from him and toward the file cabinet.

Because her knees were still on the weak side, she decided to tackle the bottom drawer first. On the floor, she began to rummage through the drawer when she realized that there was a small safe lodged at the back of the drawer.

"What do you make of this?" she asked Smith, opening the drawer all the way.

"Off hand," he deadpanned, "I'd say it was a safe."

"I know that." She frowned at the rectangular box. "Why do you think he keeps it here?"

"So that people like you and me don't find it," he answered simply.

Her conscience fought a short, mighty duel with her sense of practicality. Practicality struck a blow of victory.

"Can you get into it?"

"Only one way to find out." Lifting the safe, which was surprisingly light in comparison to many with the same dimensions, he put it on the desk. It had a simple combination lock.

He applied himself to the job at hand. Ten minutes later, it was open.

"How did you learn how to do that?" she asked in stunned surprise. Granted she'd asked him to open it, but she hadn't really thought he could.

The smile on his face was enigmatic. "You really don't want to know."

"Yes, I do." She wanted to know everything about him. Good, bad, everything.

"I did some handiwork for this private investigator. You know how most P.I.'s are former policemen?" She nodded, waiting. "This one was a former cat burglar. He paid me minimum for the work I did for him and made up the difference by teaching me a few things he thought might come in handy."

"Like breaking into safes?"

"Like opening a lock I'd forgotten the combination to."

Put that way, it made sense. She let it go and turned her attention to what the professor could have possibly had that he would put into a safe, not in a bank vault or keep at his home, but here.

There were no valuables inside, only a ledger and a sealed brown manila envelope. The ledger looked as if he was keeping a tally of different sums. There was no indication if the numbers referred to money or something else. Or even where they went. There were dates, with initials and sums, but nothing more.

"Well, that's odd," she said to Smith.

The manila envelope was even odder. In the upper right-hand corner, written in small, neat script, was Rachel's name.

"Why don't you open it?" Smith suggested.

She shook her head. It was one thing to open the safe. That was the professor's and they were trying to save the man's position. But this had Rachel's name on it. What if it belonged to her? She had no excuse for opening the envelope.

The second Smith made the suggestion, he saw the dilemma. If they tore the envelope open, Harrison would know someone had been going through his things. "We can take it with us and steam it open."

She couldn't help smiling. "Nothing more sophisticated than that?"

He shrugged carelessly. "Sometimes simple works best."

"This might not belong to the professor. It has Rachel James's name on it." She saw the name meant nothing to him. "She was a year ahead of us." There was more, but for now Jane didn't bother going into it. Into the fact that she'd always felt that Rachel had a special bond with the professor, similar and yet somehow different from her own. For one thing, she'd never seen Rachel invited to the professor's house, the way she had been countless times. "Maybe I'll just show this to Rachel and see if it's hers, or if she knows why it's in his safe."

She was confident that if there was anything inside the envelope that they could use for their cause, Rachel would let them know. Rachel was as eager to help the man as she was. She was also pretty confident that she was safe in removing the envelope. What were the odds he'd look for this just when it was missing? If anything he'd think he'd misplaced it. She made a mental note to replace the envelope as quickly as possible.

Smith shrugged. "You're the ringleader here," he quipped.

Her smile widened at the comment. They had certainly come a very long way in a very short while. Especially Smith. He'd gone from a monotoned, mono-syllabic loner to someone who was warm, funny and dependable.

As for her, well, she felt as if she was still riding a lightning bolt.

As she went back to work, she said a prayer that the sky would never clear up.

Rachel James ran a hand through her soft, curly hair as she stared at the manila envelope on her coffee table. Jane had left in her car less than ten minutes ago. The woman had called her, then dropped by with this mysterious envelope, saying she'd uncovered it during her search through the professor's private files.

Why did the professor have something with her name on it that he felt he had to keep sealed? Why wouldn't he have mentioned it to her when she'd returned to the campus?

She considered herself one of the professor's failures. He'd been her mentor while she was at school and had always taken an interest in her that she'd found comforting. But they'd had a falling out when she'd suddenly decided to drop out of school and get married. The professor'd had no way of knowing how much she'd needed to feel that someone loved her. Her adoptive parents had always been emotionally distant, almost abusive to her, making her feel that they thought they'd made a mistake, taking her in.

The professor had been the first one to try to nurture a feeling of self-worth within her. The man she'd married had brought it to fruition. But the professor had been right. She'd had no business getting married so young. Dropping out of school before earning her degree had been another mistake.

Her life was fraught with mistakes. And now, here she was, a thirty-year-old widow with next to no future. A fatal illness had claimed her husband, but not before an overwhelming amount of medical debt had been incurred. A debt she had little hope of crawling out from under. The professor slipped her money when he could, but it would take far more than that to get her out of debt.

She eyed the envelope with no small anxiety. What was inside? And why had it been kept from her?

Rachel searched for courage, afraid of what she might find. She tried to tell herself that the contents could very well just have something to do with the years she had spent at Saunders. But then why seal it? Why not just keep it in a folder, the way everyone else's records were kept?

This was ridiculous. She couldn't just sit here all night, staring at the envelope.

Taking a deep breath, Rachel took it and tore open the flap, shaking out the contents.

Her eyes widened as, after a moment, she realized she was looking at adoption papers. Her adoption papers. The pages were slightly yellowed with time. These were the originals, she thought.

What was he doing with them?

For a while now she'd been toying with the idea of finding her birth parents. The only thing that prevented her was her fear that she'd discover something she didn't want to know. But it looked now as if fate had decided to take the choice out of her hands.

Her heart pounding, she quickly scanned the pages. In the space beside "father" the word "unknown" was entered. Did that mean her birth mother slept around? That she hadn't ultimately known who the father of her baby was, or was it that she'd just been unwilling to make his identity public?

Rachel caught herself praying it was the latter.

And then she saw another entry.

Her pounding heart halted for a moment. "So that's your name," she whispered. "Rosemary Johnson." An odd feeling rippled over her. After all this time, she'd finally learned her birth mother's name. A small smile curved the corners of her mouth as she stared at the name. "Hello, Rosemary, I'm Rachel James. Your daughter."

Rachel pressed her lips together. Waves of emotion rose up into her throat, threatening to pour out. She felt like laughing and crying all at the same time.

Most of all, she felt confused.

Why would the professor have this? And then a reason suggested itself to her. Had her mother been one of Professor Harrison's students? Had he tried to help her the same way he had so many other students? The same way he had helped her countless times, giving her money, encouraging her.

"He's in trouble, you know," she whispered to the paper, still looking at her mother's name. "But we're going to help him. Somehow, we're going to find a way to help him."

Rachel had a feeling that wherever she was, Rosemary Johnson would have approved.

Smith had remained in his car while Jane stopped at Rachel's house. He didn't really know the woman and had thought it best just to keep out of the way.

But there was no question in his mind that he was going to stop over at Jane's house, at least for a little while. He was far too wired to return to the small apartment where he lived.

Besides, he still hadn't told Jane his news yet.

Danny was waiting up for them, even though it was later than usual. Smith never doubted it.

The boy bounced up into his arms in what seemed like a single bound the moment he walked into the house. He realized he'd anticipated it. More than that, he'd welcomed it.

"You came!" Danny declared.

"Sure looks that way," Smith agreed. He saw Gladys giving him a very knowing, very approving look over the boy's dark head. He nodded a greeting at her.

"Danny and I had some pizza," Gladys volunteered on her way out. "There's still some in the refrigerator." She glanced over her shoulder at Smith. "You're welcome to it if you want."

"Thank you, Gladys. I don't know what I'd do without you."

"Find yourself a man to take care of you would be my suggestion," Gladys responded, her eyes fairly twinkling, as if she'd just told herself a joke.

And then she was gone.

Jane turned away from the door and looked at her son, who had scrambled down from Smith's arms and made her think of a rubberband about to be shot into the air.

"You know, Danny…" She paused to pick up one of his toys. "Once school starts, you're not going to be able to keep these night-owl hours of yours."

Instead of pouting or protesting, both of which she anticipated, Danny surprised her by looking up at Smith. "Will you be coming home from school early, too?" Danny asked.

Jane felt her heart twist a little. Danny was assuming too much, thinking of Smith as a permanent fixture in his life. It was all well and good for her to have this fantasy about Smith, but another for Danny to invest his heart this way. How was he going to feel once Smith stopped coming around?

Funny, she didn't think of it in terms of her putting an end to what was going on. She thought of Smith as being the one to walk away. But that was because, in her heart she knew that she didn't want this to end. She admitted to herself that she would have been very happy to have Smith in her life until the last moment she drew breath.

Strange thoughts for a woman who, just a few short weeks ago had been completely convinced that she never wanted to have anything to do with another man other than her son and the professor.

Never say never, a small voice whispered in her head.

"Yeah," Smith told the boy, "Your mother'll be coming home early, too."

He was preparing to take himself out of the mix, Jane thought. The pang she felt over the thought was overwhelming. Doubly so because it affected not just her, but the person she loved the most. Her son.

"And you?" Danny pressed.

She was just about to tell him not to bother Smith when Smith replied, "And me."

Was he just humoring the boy? Or was he serious? She couldn't tell. The expression on his face made her think he was telling the truth, but that could be deceptive, as well. What she did know with a fair amount of certainty was that Danny was probably making Smith uncomfortable.

Nothing made a man run for the door faster than the threat of commitment.

"Okay," she announced, throwing another toy into the large toy box, "off to bed."

Smith smiled at her over Danny's head and mouthed the words, "Fine by me."

Afraid she was going to blush and leave herself open for a host of questions from her son, Jane lowered her eyes. And saw Danny take Smith's hand into his just before he began to lead the man off to his room.

"Danny," she chided softly, "Mr. Parker has to leave."

Smith looked at her over his shoulder. "No," he told her, "I don't."

Looking back later, she would have said that was probably the moment, if she had to pick one, that she fell in love with Smith.

Hopelessly and completely in love.

When he emerged from Danny's room some twenty minutes later, Smith was surprised to find Jane leaning against the opposite wall in the hallway, waiting for him.

"Thank you," she said as he eased the door closed.

"For?"

"For not fleeing the second Danny started making noises about you staying."

It never crossed his mind. It might have, a few weeks ago. But not anymore. He was a different person from the man he was then. And it was because of them.

"I like your son," he told her. "I never thought much about kids, one way or another, but I like your son." And then he looked at her for a long moment, really looked at her, seeing the woman beneath the surface beauty. "And I like you, too."

Her smile blossomed like wild roses after the rain. "Good to know, considering."

He knew exactly what she was thinking about. Because the lovemaking they'd experienced together had been on his mind, too.

Taking her hand much the way Danny had taken his, Smith led her to her room. She followed quietly in his wake. There was no hesitation, no momentary confusion for either of them. It was as it should have been. The way they both wanted it.

With the evening stretched ahead of them, the lovemaking was languid, allowing them to savor, to enjoy, to reexamine everything that had already been examined so many times before. To find new things.

Smith made love with her as if time had decided to stand still and he had an endless supply from which to dip into.

And once the lovemaking was over, once she lay in his arms, curled against him, feeling more content than she thought was humanly possible, he told her.

"I've decided to do what you suggested."

She looked up at him. His words had come out of the blue. "Which was?"

He wasn't aware of taking in a deep breath, but she was. She could feel it as it went in, could feel his chest moving. She didn't know what to expect.

"I've sent in my application to Saunders. I'm enrolling in the spring semester."

Jane bolted upright. "Oh, Smith, that's wonderful! I'm so proud of you."

He warmed to her embrace as her arms went around him. "Well, it's all your doing."

Jane picked up her head and looked at him, confused. "My doing?"

"Yes. I figured this way, you wouldn't be embarrassed to be seen with me."

How could he even think such a thing? "I'd never be embarrassed to be seen with you," she protested. "I'm glad you're going back, but that's because I think you have a great deal of potential and you'd be foolish not to use it." And then she frowned as his words played back in her head. "When have I ever given you any reason to think that I'd be ashamed to be seen with you? You're kind, sweet, good with small children—"

There were sparks in her eyes. Anger made her look magnificent. And he could feel himself wanting her. "And horny. Don't forget horny."

The words took the wind out of her sails. And made her grin. That would make three times, if she counted the storage room and she intended to count the storage room until her dying day.

"Again?"

He moved his shoulders in a vague shrug. "What can I say? You bring it out of me. I haven't been with a woman, other than you, in a long time and once you opened Pandora's box—"

She laughed and shook her head. "Weak in literature, I see. You're going to need tutoring. The professor would have been sadly disappointed if he'd heard you just now."

Confused, Smith gave her a puzzled look. "I don't follow."

"When Pandora opened the box, all sorts of evil things flew out into the world." She touched his face, thinking that she had never felt so in love as she did this very moment. "There isn't one evil thing about this."

It was the last thing she said just before she kissed him. And initiated another exquisite round of lovemaking.

Chapter Fourteen

A week later, as he was crossing the grounds, Smith stopped dead.

Just one heartbeat ago, he'd felt as close to being invincible as he'd ever had. He had his life back on track again. Finally applying to go back to school to get his degree meant he was that much closer to becoming an independent business owner.

The thought of having his own landscaping business wasn't merely just a pipe dream anymore. At long last it was on its way to becoming a reality.

And, as an added bonus, there was finally someone in his life he really cared about. Someone who made life worth the effort.

But right at this moment, his breath had left his body, making him hallucinate.

That had to be it.

He couldn't possibly be seeing who he thought he saw. With this much distance between them, features tended to blur. Besides, it had been nine years. Nine years since he'd last laid eyes on the man who'd been ultimately responsible for derailing his life.

Jacob Weber.

People change in nine years, they look different…

Even so, he was dead certain that it was Weber. Wasn't the professor actively seeking out former students who he could point to with the pride of an educator who had helped guide them onto the path of success? And nobody matched that status better than Weber. The vain, pompous Weber had become not just a doctor, but a famous one. He enjoyed no small measure of renown as a highly successful fertility specialist.

Smith watched as the crisp, late summer breeze ruffled the man's thick, dark chestnut hair and felt his heart harden.

It was Weber, all right.

A high-pitched squeal behind him had Smith swinging around to look, only to see two young women excitedly coming together, hugging and laughing, both talking at once.

Probably comparing their summers, he guessed. When he turned back, he saw that Weber was looking directly at him. From the look on the man's handsome face, Weber was obviously trying to decide the same thing he had just been wrestling with.

And then he started to walk across the newly mowed expanse of grass, right toward him.

Smith instantly braced himself for some sort of a confrontation. The last time he and Weber had seen one another, it had literally come to blows. People on the campus had jumped in to separate them. Their faces were a blur then. All he remembered was Weber's. He wasn't even sure who had initiated the confrontation, only that Weber had had the beating coming to him.

It was Weber, incredibly paranoid about having his secret brought to light, who had gone to the university's financial administrators to swear that, he, Jacob Weber, had seen one Smith Parker sneaking out of the girls' section of the dorm after having taken several valuable items from their rooms.

The stolen items were never found, but Smith had a strong suspicion he knew where they were, or at least where they had been taken. To some out-of-the-way pawn shop. By Weber himself.

Because Weber had come from a rich family while Smith had been raised in a working class family that barely got by, the university officials had believed what Weber had told them. It seemed oddly ironic that Weber had been so dedicated to getting him kicked out for the very thing Weber might have done himself. Because Smith had seen Weber coming out of a pawn shop a couple of times, always pocketing money.

A little sleuthing, brought on by a heavy dose of curiosity and an innate desire to protect himself, had revealed to him that Jacob Weber wasn't what he seemed. The silver spoon that everyone knew he'd been born with had, because of shameful circumstances, long since been wrenched out of his mouth.

The money that Weber enjoyed bragging about so much had all been lost by a father who was the victim of an overwhelming gambling addiction. The same father who subsequently walked out on Weber and his mother. The latter was no prize, either. Weber's mother spent more time communing with her bottle of the moment than she did with the son she'd given birth to.

Weber had spent a good deal of his time looking over his shoulder as he went through complicated machinations to perpetrate the aura of being the favored only son of an obscenely wealthy couple. To protect the lie and prevent anyone from learning the embarrassing truth, Weber had done everything he could to get Smith thrown out before he told anyone where the Weber money was really coming from in those days. From pawned items that he had either stolen from strangers or from his own mother.

Striking before he was struck, Weber had taken his fabricated story to the administrators and they had suspended the scholarship that Smith had so desperately needed to continue going to school. Wounded that Weber's word was taken over his without so much as the benefit of the doubt, something had happened to him. He'd lost the will to defend himself, sinking into the depression that led to his dropping out. Out of school and, temporarily, out of life.

Weber had won his victory.

And now, after all this time, their paths were about to cross again. Well, he wasn't that same idealistic, wet-behind-the-ears kid he'd been then. He might never become a famous anything, the way Weber was, but he had the same right to be happy as Weber did. And no one was ever going to take that away from him again. He wouldn't allow it.

Smith braced himself, acutely aware that he was standing dressed in the navy-blue coveralls of a Saunders university maintenance worker while Jacob Weber was wearing a custom-made suit that probably amounted to at least two months of his salary.

Once that would have made him self-conscious, now his uniform became his badge of courage. At least he knew that he wasn't a liar.

"It *is* you," Jacob declared in hushed surprise when he was less than five feet away from him. "Smith Parker." He said the name as if to solidify past and present.

Standing his ground, Smith nodded curtly at him. "Weber."

"It's Dr. Weber now." Jacob made the correction automatically. His voice was surprisingly devoid of any of that telltale bravado that had been its hallmark when they'd attended Saunders.

Smith saw the man's dark blue eyes sweep over him. Probably finding what to criticize next. He squared his shoulders. "I heard."

All around them were the sounds of a campus waking up from a long summer's nap, preparing to launch itself full-bore into the fall term. Clusters of students were greeting other students and conversations were breaking out all around the circle of silence as the two men stood warily regarding one another. One an obvious success, the other not.

* * *

As Jacob looked at the man he'd once considered a threat, a potential enemy, the quills of guilt brushed sharply against his conscience. Smith Parker, a man he knew was very intelligent, had gone on to become a man who wielded nothing more challenging than a mop and a plunger for a living.

It was harsh, coming face-to-face with the consequence of his actions. And the consequence here was that, because of his own petty vanity and monumental insecurity, he had been instrumental in ruining a man's life.

The healer within Jacob felt the sharp, bitter sting of guilt.

He wished he had it to do over again.

Jacob shifted a little uneasily, his eyes never leaving Smith's face. "Look, would you like to grab a drink at the Hub?"

Driving onto the campus, he'd seen that the old student hang-out, sporting a brand-new coat of paint but retaining its old logo, was still very much a fixture. When he had attended Saunders, the Hub had been where everyone met to grab a couple of slices of pizza and a mug of beer. To talk, chill out and not think about school for a few hours.

Smith, he remembered, had worked there, too, to earn a few extra dollars.

"With you?" Smith asked coldly. "No."

Smith had every intention of leaving Weber standing there when he began walking away. But then he thought he heard the man say something. Temper on edge, he turned around again and looked at Weber.

"What did you say?"

Weber cleared his throat as if the words had gotten stuck there, weren't something he was accustomed to uttering. "I said, I'm sorry. Sorry I got you thrown out."

Smith congratulated himself on concealing his surprise well. "You didn't," he said, not giving him the satisfaction. "I got myself thrown out."

About to leave, Smith found himself wavering. He had a lunch break coming and there was nothing pressing on his work list at the moment. He was more than caught up. He made sure of it so that there as nothing to interfere with his helping Jane.

Jane.

It was her influence that had him even considering this. That had him silently accepting Weber's apology.

With a careless shrug, he said, "I guess I can spare a few minutes."

A nervous smile quirked Jacob's mouth. Ordinarily, a high-handed remark like that would likely have angered him, but he obviously felt he needed to make at least a few amends for his sins.

And what he had done to Parker remained one of his greatest offenses.

"I'd appreciate it," he said to Smith.

Despite Weber's congenial expression, Smith's radar had gone up, putting him on the alert. The Jacob Weber he knew was not kind, was not considerate. The man he remembered from his brief college stint was a self-centered, egotistical bastard out to destroy anyone who got in his way, no matter who it was. He trusted Weber just about as far as he could throw him.

Less.

Forty minutes later Smith had to concede that the man in front of him at the circular table for two they'd staked out at the Hub appeared to be trying really hard to make amends. To bury the man he had once been.

He lifted the mug of beer to his lips and drank as he regarded Weber. Because of Jane, Smith couldn't help wondering if the new leaf the man was struggling to turn over was the result of some outside force coming to bear on his life.

Smith knew that because of Jane's influence, he could now find it in his heart to forgive the man he had always blamed for the bad turn his life had wound up taking. And he realized now that what he'd initially said to Weber in an unguarded moment was true. Weber wasn't responsible for his leaving Saunders, *he* was. Just as he was taking responsibility for getting himself back in after all this time.

The mug of beer, his second, stood still full in front of him. Jacob regarded it for a moment before raising his eyes to Smith's. "So you're okay with this? With what went down between us?"

"I'm not okay with it," Smith contradicted firmly, "but I can put it behind me."

Finally, a small voice in his head declared.

Smith knew that the reason he could put the event behind him was that he was finally getting on with his life.

Jacob leaned over the small table. "You don't know

how much this means to me," he confided in an uncharacteristic moment of fellowship.

"Yeah, well, don't do it again," Smith quipped. He glanced at his watch. His lunch was almost over. He still had enough time to swing by Jane's office to see how she was doing. He pushed his chair away from the table. "I've got to be getting back."

Jacob had come, rather reluctantly, in response to Harrison's repeated calls and entreaties to go before the university board and make a statement about his time here at Saunders. Specifically about Harrison's influence on the ultimate course of his life. It was that which had gotten him thinking about the way he'd behaved while attending the university.

When he'd seen Parker crossing the grounds, it almost seemed as though fate had whispered in his ear, telling him to own up to his mistakes and to try to be a better man. Now that he'd taken the first step, it didn't seem so bad.

He had no idea how long he was going to be asked to stay, or how long he'd actually agree to. He hadn't even gone to see the professor yet. Jacob knew he had no real friends here. This could possibly be construed as his first step in that direction.

He pushed back his own chair and looked at Smith. "Maybe we could do this again sometime?"

The man's tone gave him away. It struck Smith that more than likely Weber didn't have any friends. Just as he hadn't—until Jane.

Funny, coming from two very different arenas in life like they did, in a way, they were still very much alike. Go figure.

"Maybe," Smith allowed, leaving the door ajar for the time being. He started to reach into his pocket.

"I've got it," Jacob declared, taking out a twenty and a ten. Between them, they'd ordered four mugs of beer. It didn't even amount to eight dollars a piece.

"I pay my own way," Smith informed him evenly. He took out a ten and put it on the table.

Jacob withdrew his hand, raising it as if to say he meant no offense. Their eyes met. There was, Smith noted, a note of respect in the other man's eyes.

"I'm sure you do," Jacob replied.

Smith left the Hub before Jacob.

She'd just gotten out of the shower less than ten minutes ago, a few beads of water still drying on her arm. She was about to check on dinner when she heard the doorbell.

He was early.

She'd told Smith to come at five and it wasn't even four-thirty. She wasn't ready. Thank God, Gladys had volunteered to take Danny over to his friend's house for his sleepover or else she would have probably been standing here, still naked.

But then, considering what she had in mind for tonight, that might not have been such a bad thing. Jane smiled to herself. Tonight was going to be all about them. For tonight, she wasn't going to be Danny's mom or Professor Harrison's crusading assistant, she was going to be Jane Jackson, all female, and completely in love.

Okay, so he was early. That meant that he couldn't wait. She could deal with that.

Wearing a bright smile, incredibly sexy underwear and a dress that whispered promises as it hugged her curves, Jane opened the door.

The second she saw Smith, a burst of sunshine swept over her.

The next second, warning lights went off. Something was wrong. He looked different.

He looked, she realized, the way he had before they'd began seeing one another.

Mustering her courage, she tried to remain cheerful. "You're early," she commented as she closed the door. The dark, impassive expression on his face sent a chill over her heart. She dropped the pretense as she took his hand. "What's the matter?"

Smith pulled his hand away, creating a chasm between them. Even now, just a few steps into her house, he considered not telling her. When he'd first opened up the envelope and read what was inside, old habits kicked in. He'd immediately withdrawn into himself. When ill—and this made him ill—animals crawled into some enclosure to weather what they had, or die. He'd been doing the same for a long time.

But now there was this incredible ache in the pit of his stomach that he just couldn't keep to himself, couldn't seem to handle alone.

He needed an outlet of some kind to help him cope.

So he had come here, where he'd come to believe he was supposed to be. But he was here now and he still didn't know what to do with himself, didn't even know how to frame the words that felt so hurtful inside.

Finally the words just came to the surface on their own. "They rejected me."

She stared at him, confused. Was there something going on in his department? He never mentioned his boss, so she had no idea if Smith got along with him or not. "Who rejected you?"

Smith spat the words out. "The university."

From inside his pants' pocket, he took out the letter he'd gotten in the late afternoon mail. He pushed the single printed page into her hand, then shoved his own into his pockets and began to pace. He was a portrait of frustration.

"They said because of my 'past performance,' they couldn't let me reenter the academic program. 'Past performance,'" he repeated angrily. "One damn, lousy semester, that's all it was. The rest of the grades were more than acceptable. I had a 3.5 GPA until that last semester."

Her heart pounding, Jane looked at the letter. The paper was all crinkled, as if someone had crumpled it up into a ball before thinking better of it and rescuing it from wherever it had been thrown. She quickly read the formal language that capriciously sliced through all of Smith's budding hopes.

Damn them.

She looked up at Smith. "This isn't right."

He took the letter from her. His hand closed over the page, crumpling it again, and this time, he left it that way.

"Damn straight it isn't right," he declared heatedly. "But it's the way things are." He laughed shortly. Dismissively. The sound went right through her. "I was a fool to think I could go back. A fool to think I could do something with my life—"

For a second, just a second, she thought of letting him vent, of letting Smith say the terrible things he was saying because he was so frustrated at the unfairness of it all.

But the love she felt for him pushed her forward, put words into her mouth.

"No, damn it, you *weren't* a fool. *Aren't* a fool," she corrected herself, her voice trembling with indignation at the unfair treatment he was receiving. "They're the ones who are the fools for turning you down."

"Yeah, well, I don't think that's really going to bother them very much." He bit the words off, still pacing.

She matched him step for step, trying to show her support in every way she could think of.

"The hell with them," she declared. When her words brought a surprised look from him, she continued, "Saunders isn't the only place you can apply. There are other colleges."

And other disappointments, he thought. Didn't she see how futile it all was? "What's the point? They'll see my grades and then—"

She'd been around the administration office long enough to know where he was going with this. And he had a point. But it could be gotten around.

"Okay, for now, start at a two-year college. They'd be glad to take you. And you can always transfer credits to an accredited four year college once you get your momentum back." The eyes that were looking at her were dark. Flat. She felt like a cheerleader in a cemetery. She just wasn't getting through to him. "There're lots of ways to get there, Smith," she insisted.

He wasn't in the mood for this. Jane didn't understand. She hadn't just gotten the rug pulled out from under her. He'd never dreamed they wouldn't take him. To him, it had just been a matter of finding the time to apply and go.

"Yeah, lots of ways to get shot down," he retorted heatedly.

"But you won't be," she told him with feeling. "You're a fighter." But first he had to believe in himself. Otherwise, nothing mattered.

He stared out the window at the darkness. Black, just like his mood. Just like his future.

"I'm tired of fighting against the system," he told her reflection in the glass. "And the system says the underdog isn't going anywhere." He snorted. "Nice guys finish last and all that garbage."

Her temper flared. He just couldn't give up. Not now. Not just when he was getting himself together.

"That's just what it is, garbage," she shot back. How did she make him see what she saw? Frustration ate away at her. "Smith, you have it in you to show them they're wrong."

"Stop it," he told her harshly. "You're living in a dreamworld. And maybe it's my fault, I sure as hell should have known better, but somehow you pulled me into it, too."

A sense of horror exploded inside her chest. He was blaming her. Just like Drew, he was blaming her. She looked away, refusing to look into his eyes, afraid of the pain that lay ahead.

She couldn't go through this again, she couldn't go through loving someone only to discover she'd make a mistake. That he didn't love her the way she loved him. That he didn't really love at all.

"Maybe it's this place. Maybe I should just pick up and start all over again somewhere else." The corners of Smith's mouth looked as if they'd been welded permanently downward. His temper had reached an explosive point and he didn't want to take it out on Jane. "I'd better go."

She squared her shoulders, a soldier looking down the barrel of a gun. A protest hovered on her lips, but she didn't release it. Despite her hopes, this wasn't working out.

She felt dead inside.

"Maybe you'd better," she agreed.

Her acquiescence took him by surprise. He'd expected at least some kind of protest. When he finally brought himself to leave a few moments later, he went without saying another word. Left with a colossal sense of disappointment.

Because somewhere in his heart, he'd expected her to talk him out of it. To mount some kind of an outlandish pep rally, the kind that only she could pull together, to force him back on track again.

But maybe she was seeing things more clearly than he was. Maybe she knew, as he should have, that in the end, it was hopeless. His life was set on a course that couldn't be altered. This was all there was.

The sooner he got used to that, the sooner he could stop believing in the impossible. There was no Santa Claus, no tooth fairy, no second chance.

Not for him.

She heard Smith start up his car. Heard it as it pulled away from her driveway.

Away from her.

Only then did she give in to the tears.

It was over.

Chapter Fifteen

Jane had no recollection of bonelessly sliding against the door onto the floor.

Nor did she have any idea how long she remained there, hugging her knees against her chest, sobbing. With Danny out of the house, she didn't have to put up a brave front, the way she did every time there'd been a flare-up with Drew.

She cried her heart out. Because it was broken and of no further use to her.

Spent, exhausted, her head ached and her throat felt almost raw. She probably would have fallen asleep there if it hadn't been for the noise.

The thudding sound against her back penetrated only when it started becoming more intense.

Someone was banging on her door.

Jane snapped to attention. The first thing she thought of was Danny. Something had happened to Danny.

"Just—just a minute."

The tears in her throat were all but choking her. Wiping the wet tracks on her cheeks away with the back of her hand, she dragged a hand through her hair, pushing it off her face. Then she pulled herself up to her feet and yanked open the door without bothering to ask who it was.

She took her breath in sharply. Smith was on her doorstop.

A torrent of emotions rose up inside her. Jane felt torn between wanting to throw herself into his arms and wanting to beat on him with doubled-up fists. Constrained, she did neither.

Instead she raised her head proudly and asked in a voice as devoid of emotion as possible, "Forget something?"

He'd meant to stay away forever. Forever had lasted less than an hour.

That was how long it had taken for him to come to his senses. An hour. He'd driven back like a man possessed, trying to figure out what words to say to undo what he'd done.

The second he saw her, guilt riddled through him like bullets being fired from a hair-triggered automatic weapon. Smith cursed himself. He was responsible for this. She deserved so much better and he'd done this to her. He was going to make it up to her if it took him the rest of his life.

"Yeah," he answered, acutely aware that Jane wasn't opening the door any further, wasn't stepping to the side to let him in. "All the good times. I had no right to yell at you like that."

"No," she replied quietly, "you didn't."

The sadness in her voice ripped him apart. "Would it help to say I was sorry?"

She doubted the words had a familiar taste in his mouth. To say them had to be very difficult for him.

"It would be a start." After a beat, she stepped aside, letting him come in.

He brushed a kiss against her cheek, relieved at the second chance. Smith wanted her to understand why he'd behaved so badly. It wasn't an excuse, but it was a reason.

"I just got so damn frustrated. I finally was doing something positive with my life and I got knocked down again by the so-called sins of my past—"

She knew that there was a stigma that went beyond his one semester of poor grades. Mentally shrugging off the last effects of her crying jag, she got back into fighting form. "We need to have the record set straight. Once and for all. You're not a thief, you didn't take those things. Anyone who knows you would know that."

That was the trouble. No one who had been part of the administration process, then or now, knew him. But back then, they'd known Jacob Weber. Or thought they had. No one would have believed him if he'd said that Weber was probably the one who'd taken the missing items because he'd needed the money. No one would believe him now. The only one who could set this right was Weber.

But even though Weber had apologized the other day, Smith knew the man wouldn't risk the bad publicity that confessing to this sort of misdeed might generate.

Smith sighed. He wasn't about to climb up higher by using the body of another man as a stepping stone. That wasn't who he was.

"Water under the bridge, Jane." He saw that she wasn't content to just let it continue flowing. She opened her mouth to protest, but he already had an alternative solution. "I guess I'll give what you suggested a shot—go to a two year college and then try to transfer."

He'd said something else that had her worried. "Then, you're not leaving Boston?"

Blurting that out had been nothing short of stupid on his part, he thought.

"No, because if I did, I'd be leaving the best thing that ever happened to me." Smith pulled her into his arms. To his relief, she didn't resist. Didn't hold what he'd done against him. His mouth curved into a soft smile as he brushed his fingers along her cheek, tracing the ghost of a tear stain. "I made you cry."

She shook her head, her lips twitching in that smile he'd learned to love so well. "No, I was just peeling onions."

Smith raised one of her hands to his nose and sniffed. "No onion smell."

"New kind of onion," she deadpanned, slipping her hand from his and dropping it to her side. "The farmers are very excited about it."

He pulled her closer. "Not half as excited as I am about you."

She could tell where this was leading. Where they both wanted it to. To her bedroom. She glanced toward the kitchen. "What about dinner?"

Smith pressed a kiss to the side of her neck that made her pulse scramble and her breathing grow short. *The hell with dinner,* she thought. She was a great deal hungrier for the feel of his body than she was for anything she could put on a plate.

"It'll keep," he told her.

There was laughter in her eyes. "I guess it will at that."

He swept her up into his arms and carried her to her room where, for the rest of the evening, he tried to make up for what he had done not only to her, but to himself as well.

He enjoyed a remarkably high success rate.

Jane was very aware that the school year was galloping closer and closer and that they—she, Sandra and Rachel—had a limited amount of time left to mount a successful campaign to keep the professor in his present position. She and Smith worked through the files diligently, garnering as much information as they could.

She passed a great deal on to the other women, and kept a large number for herself, combing through the files intently. Looking for anything that they could use.

She was at it every moment she could spare and had a host of papers spread out on her desk now, when she should have been at lunch.

Most of her lunches were spent this way, leaving her evenings free to search for more files and her nights free to be with Smith.

Right now, she'd found something that might or might not be useful. In any event, it seemed like a very odd coincidence. She shuffled through several papers, pages she'd downloaded from her scanner and then printed up. It looked as if many of the students who she knew the professor would have considered to be his prize students were the recipients of mysterious allocations of money.

She had in front of her copies of letters she'd found in their files at the administration office, saying that certain funds were being held in trust for them, to be used in conjunction with their schooling.

Just like the letter she'd received, she thought.

For many of the students, the money meant the difference between dropping out of school and going on to receive their diplomas.

Just like her, she thought again.

Jane flipped through the letters she'd pulled. Nowhere was there any mention of where the money had come from, or why. If this had involved some sort of official university-backed scholarship, she was certain that it would have been referred to as such. Someone's name or logo would have been affixed to it instead of just having the money labeled as "funds."

This definitely bore further investigation, Jane thought. At the very least, she wanted to see if any of the students who weren't directly or indirectly associated with the professor had received this kind of mysterious financial aid. Finding out one way or another probably wasn't going to be much help to the professor, but her curiosity had been aroused. She felt she needed to get to the bottom of this.

"You need to have more fun."

Jane jumped at her desk, startled. She'd been so absorbed wondering about this unlikely coincidence, she hadn't seen the professor peeking in from the hall, or even heard him.

Before answering, she quickly scooped together the papers that were on her desk, then struggled to look nonchalant as she deposited them in the yellow folder. She prayed that he thought she was going about a little personal business during her lunchtime.

"I have my share," she finally said.

The professor crossed the threshold and looked at her. "Smith?" he guessed, then chuckled when he saw color rise to her cheeks. "How is he?"

Wonderful. The word echoed in her head as she thought of last night. She concentrated on giving an accurate reply to his question. "Frustrated right now."

There was immediate interest in the man's eyes. That was what she loved about him. He cared about everyone he came in contact with. "How so?"

She knew that Smith probably would have rather she kept the story to herself, but it made her angry every time she thought about it. It was so unfair. "I actually got him to apply to Saunders in order to finally get his diploma—"

The professor's face lit up, erasing some of the weariness that was etched there. "Wonderful!"

But she shook her head. "Not so wonderful. The school rejected him."

He looked at her, the words not quite computing. "Rejected him?" The professor came closer, as if proximity might promote understanding. "Why?"

She sighed, struggling to rein in her anger. "Because his grades the last semester he attended Saunders were so poor. They were only like that because—"

"He was upset about the allegations. Yes, I know." Smith had abruptly left the university before he could try to help him. Gilbert paused, thinking. "Someone needs to have a talk with the powers that be." He said the words more to himself than to her.

Jane felt alarmed. "Professor, you're in a tenuous enough position as it is," she warned. "I didn't mean to make you think that I wanted you to do something about getting Smith admitted. He—"

Gilbert raised his hand, cutting her protest short. "If I won't do my job because I'm afraid of losing it, then there's no point in my keeping my job, is there?"

She admired his integrity, she always had. But everything had a time and place and discretion was still the better part of valor. "Does the term 'lay low' mean anything to you, Professor?"

Gilbert moved toward the door. His eyes twinkled as he looked back at her just before he left. "Sorry, I was never up on slang."

Jane blew out a breath. God, what had she just done? It felt as if things were only getting worse.

Her stomach refused to untie itself from the knot that threatened to send her off to an urgent, face-to-face meeting with the porcelain bowl in her bathroom. It had felt this way ever since Smith had called her in her office. He hadn't come in person, just called on her telephone. She couldn't help but take it as a bad sign, even though Smith hadn't sounded down when he'd called. He told her that he would meet her at her house.

The instructions were that she and Danny were to dress up because he was taking them out.

Had he changed his mind? Was this going to be a farewell dinner?

Try as she might to cling to this newfound happiness that had entered her life, the woman she'd been, the one who had suffered setback after emotional setback, even as she was being pulled up to her feet by the professor, was afraid that everything was going to abruptly end. That Smith had changed his mind again. About school.

About her.

What was she going to do if she was right?

Lacing her fingers together in front of her, she glanced at Danny. She'd just finished helping him get dressed over loud protests that he didn't like being fancy. Only when she told him that Smith had asked him to dress up did he stop complaining.

The boy worshipped Smith. Another mistake on her part? She looked at him now. He was watching the door as anxiously as she was.

Please don't tell me you're leaving me. Leaving us.

She had no contingency plan, nothing to fall back on if she was right. She'd never prayed so hard to be wrong in her life.

And then, suddenly, the doorbell was ringing and

her heart was threatening to jump ship and leave her to sink or swim on her own.

Taking a deep breath, telling herself that she was ready for anything, knowing that she was lying, Jane went to the front door, nearly colliding with Danny who'd raced to it, as well. After a second, Danny stepped back.

Jane opened the door.

The next second she found herself being scooped up and spun around in a wide circle.

"Me, next," Danny cried, sounding like the typical five-year-old he wasn't. He raised up his arms to Smith. "Me, next."

Kissing her soundly, Smith deposited her back down on the floor.

"Okay, you next!" he declared, picking up the boy and whirling him high in the air. Danny's giggles filled the room.

He was staying. A man didn't come into a woman's house and twirl both her and her son around as if they were rag dolls if he meant to walk out on them. Did he?

"What is this all about?" Jane asked, catching her breath.

For the first time since he'd sat in the same classroom with her, she saw Smith grin from ear to ear. He stood back for her benefit, his arms out to the side.

"You are now looking at a future Saunders University graduate." There was no mistaking the pride in his voice.

Or in her heart, either. She stared at him, afraid that she'd misheard. "You got accepted?"

Smith nodded his head smartly. "I got accepted," he confirmed.

Just a few days ago, the world had looked so bleak. She knew he'd had his heart set on graduating from Saunders. And now it looked as if it was going to finally happen. "When? How? Did you reapply?"

"Today. I'm not sure and no." Almost reverently, he took the letter he'd brought for her to see out of his jacket pocket and handed it to her. "This came in my mail today."

He'd gone home during lunch because he'd forgotten something and, on a whim, since he'd just seen the mail carrier leave, had checked his mailbox. He couldn't believe his good luck. Keeping this from Jane, even for a few hours, had been hard.

Jane read the letter quickly. It was from the administration, saying that it had come to their attention that special circumstances had been brought to bear during his final semester at Saunders. Because of the nature of those circumstances, they were going to disallow the grades from that time period. Which brought him up to a 3.5 index and that was more than acceptable by the standards Saunders University had set for its admissions. In addition, further examination of the underlying circumstances had made them decide to reinstate his scholarship.

Her mouth dropped open. It was like reading about a miracle. She blinked several times, but the words on the page didn't change.

She looked at Smith. "You're in."

Saying it was going to take some getting used to, he thought. He still half expected someone to come and tell him it was all a joke.

"I'm in."

Danny had been shifting impatiently from foot to foot. He didn't like being excluded from anything. "In what?" he wanted to know.

"Heaven," Smith declared. And none of this would have ever come about, he knew, if it hadn't been for Jane. If she hadn't made him want to try in the first place. He knew that no matter how this had managed to arrange itself, he had her to thank for everything.

Danny frowned at Smith, confused. "But if you're there and we can see you, then we're there, too." He looked from Smith to his mother. "Are we dead?"

Smith laughed. The kid was always thinking. "I see I'm going to need all the education I can get just to keep up with this boy."

Jane replayed his words in her head, wondering if he knew what he'd just implied. That he intended to be part of their lives for more than just the week.

It was safer just to concentrate on what he'd said about Danny. She laughed, looking at her son. "I'm thinking of taking some night courses myself."

Smith looked serious and she couldn't tell if he was pretending or if he meant it when he said, "We might have to work out a schedule then."

Was he saying what she thought he was saying? That he wanted to go on seeing her. Perhaps even on a not-so-casual basis? Toying with the thought, her heart refused to settled down.

Because of what she'd gone through these last few days, she decided that entitled her to be a little coy. "Why?"

"So that one of us will always be home for Danny." He

ruffled the boy's hair, hooking his arm around Danny's neck, he pulled him closer. Danny was eating it up.

"Home for Danny," she echoed. Pulling Smith aside, Jane lowered her voice, "You make it sound as if you're moving in."

He looked unfazed by her accusation. "Well, husbands and wives usually live in the same house. Unless they're bi-coastal, but I think that's too much separation, don't you?" He didn't give her a chance to answer. "A few hours a day is more than enough to—"

"Smith, Smith, wait. Wait," she cried. To underscore her plea, she put her fingertips on his lips. "Did I just miss something here?" She didn't need that answered. She knew she must have. "What are you saying?"

He framed her face for a moment, thinking how beautiful she was. And how lucky he was that she had come back into his life.

"You didn't miss anything because I'm jumping around. And I'm jumping around because this is all new to me. Being happy isn't something I'm really accustomed to." He stopped himself before he rambled on. Taking a breath, he posed a question to her that, as far as he saw, put everything into focus. "How would you like me to tend your garden on a permanent basis?"

He'd thought wrong. Jane wasn't following him at all. "You're applying to be my gardener?"

Gardener was part of it, he supposed. He looked forward to teaching her. "More than that if you'll let me."

His voice was echoing in her head, with sound bits of his words going everywhere. And then her eyes opened wide. How in heaven's name had she missed that the first time around? "Does this have something to do with the 'husband and wife' reference?"

"It has everything to do with the husband and wife reference." He didn't like putting himself on the line. But there was no other way to do this. Sometimes life demanded risks.

Taking her hand, he led her back to a very curious Danny. His fingers still laced with hers, he took one of Danny's hands in his free one.

"Now what? Do we sing 'Kum-ba-ya'?" she asked.

"Now I do this." And as he said it, Smith got down on one knee.

"Is this a game?" Danny began to mimic Smith, but his mother pulled him back.

"Oh, God, I hope not," Jane whispered, her eyes on Smith.

He had his answer, Smith thought. Prayed. But the question needed to be asked anyway.

"Jane, Danny—" he looked at each of them as he said their names "—my life has gotten infinitely better since you came into it. I love you both."

"We love you, too," Danny declared.

"Danny," Jane cried.

"Well, we do. I do. Don't you?" he asked his mother.

Smith looked at her, the same question in his eyes that was on Danny's lips. She couldn't hold it in any longer. "Yes, I love him."

Smith had never known that he could feel this relieved. "Then will you and Danny do me the supreme honor of marrying me?" he asked.

"I get to marry you, too?" Danny cried, elated.

Smith looked at Jane. "Only if your mom says yes."

Fairly jumping up and down now, Danny looked at her, his voice pleading. "Say yes, Mom, say yes!"

Her eyes softened. "If I don't, I'll never hear the end of it."

"That's a promise," Smith told her. "Because in this case, I don't intend to take no for an answer."

If her heart had any more love in it, she was fairly certain that it would have exploded. "Then I won't give it."

Danny wasn't sure if that was enough. He was taking no chances. "Say yes, Mom, say yes!" he insisted.

"Yes," she cried, then threw her arms around Smith's neck. "Yes!"

Danny followed suit, adding his small body to the pile-on. Overjoyed at being embraced by his about-to-be new dad, as well. Even if the guy was kissing his mom.

Epilogue

A story had brought him here.

He had a nose for news, as they used to say in the trade years before he was ever born. And as he got out of his car and looked around at the picturesque campus grounds that could have fronted every single movie about college life ever made, something told Ian Beck that there was a story here.

More than just a human interest one, he was willing to bet, although there was no underestimating the public's reaction to a good tug on the old heartstrings.

Revered Professor Found To Have Outlived His Usefulness, Out Of Step In A Fast-Paced, Ungrateful World Determined To Shake Him Off.

Ian took a breath, looking around at the various

groups of students, milling around or sitting on the grass. Took him back, he thought as he ran his hand through his dark brown hair. At thirty-six, he rarely got nostalgic anymore. He allowed himself a moment, remembering what it was like, being that young.

Had he ever been that young? Probably not. There were times Ian felt as if he'd been born old. Old and jaded.

Maybe it would do him some good to turn this into a human interest story.

He'd heard that the professor in question, a Gilbert Harrison, was not going to out with a gentle smile on his lips. The old boy was going to put up a fight.

Good for you, man.

He liked that. It gave the article he was framing—or maybe the series of articles, he wasn't sure yet—some spice. Everyone loved an underdog who was a fighter. And this story pitted a kindly, well-regarded, well-loved professor against the machinery of a college determined to streamline itself to draw in the best potential athletes in the country. Future hall-of-famers to line their walls.

That translated into big bucks for the university. He was fully aware of how men like Alex Broadstreet, the current president of the university's Board of Directors, operated. Not that he faulted them. You needed money to exist in this modern world. Money and lots of it. But you also needed heart and that was where the professor came in.

Or maybe it would turn out that the old boy had feet of clay. If he did, so much the better. The only thing the public liked better than having their heartstrings tugged was a full-blown scandal to sink their teeth into. The juicier, the better.

Whichever way the story took him, Ian thought, he was willing to go.

* * * * *

Don't miss the next book in
the new Special Edition continuity,
MOST LIKELY TO…
THE PREGNANCY PROJECT
by bestselling author Victoria Pade
A fertility doctor's gruff exterior is soon worn away
by a tenacious—and beautiful—
new patient, until an old scandal intrudes
on their happiness…and brings his
secrets to the surface!
Available October 2005,
only from Silhouette Books.

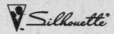

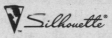

SPECIAL EDITION™

Don't miss the latest book from

Sharon De Vita

coming in October 2005!

ABOUT THE BOY

Silhouette Special Edition #1715

When widow Katie Murphy moved back to Cooper's Cove to run the newspaper, she sought a role model for her sun, Rusty. Police chief Lucas Porter proved to be the perfect mentor—but relations between Katie and Lucas weren't smooth. Could the redheaded reporter overcome Lucas's distrust of the media…and earn a press pass to his heart?

Available at your favorite retail outlet.

Where love comes alive™

eHARLEQUIN.com

The Ultimate Destination for Women's Fiction

Visit eHarlequin.com's Bookstore today
for today's most popular books at great prices.

- An extensive selection of romance books by top authors!

- Choose our convenient "bill me" option. No credit card required.

- New releases, Themed Collections and hard-to-find backlist.

- A sneak peek at upcoming books.

- Check out book excerpts, book summaries and Reader Recommendations from other members and post your own too.

- Find out what everybody's reading in Bestsellers.

- Save BIG with everyday discounts and exclusive online offers!

- Our Category Legend will help you select reading that's exactly right for you!

- Visit our Bargain Outlet often for huge savings and special offers!

- Sweepstakes offers. Enter for your chance to win special prizes, autographed books and more.

**Your purchases are 100%
guaranteed—so shop online
at www.eHarlequin.com today!**

HARLEQUIN Next™

COME OCTOBER

by *USA TODAY* bestselling author Patricia Kay

Victim of a devastating car accident, Claire Sherman couldn't bring herself to face the perfect fiancé and perfect life she'd lost. Starting over with a brand-new identity seemed like the best way to heal—but was it?

Available this October

TheNextNovel.com

Four new titles available each month at your favorite retail outlet.

SILHOUETTE *Romance*®

Is Proud to Present

JUDY Christenberry's
The Texan's Tiny
Dilemma

(Silhouette Romance #1782)

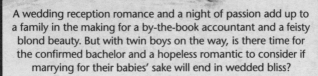

A wedding reception romance and a night of passion add up to a family in the making for a by-the-book accountant and a feisty blond beauty. But with twin boys on the way, is there time for the confirmed bachelor and a hopeless romantic to consider if marrying for their babies' sake will end in wedded bliss?

Lone Star *Brides* Don't miss this second title in Judy Christenberry's new Silhouette Romance series—LONE STAR BRIDES, and discover Mike Schofield and Teresa Tyler's enchanting happily-ever-after love story.

Available September 2005 at your favorite retail outlet.

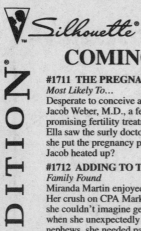

Silhouette®

COMING NEXT MONTH

SSECNM0905